Miracles

&

Misfits

Short Stories

by

Harry Castle

Author of FUGITIVE ROMANCE: The Fictional
Memoir of a Hollywood Screenwriter

Illustrations by Christiane

Why does the past seem so magical,
so…full of miracles and light?
John Banville

The future ain't what it used to be.

Yogi Berra

Stories

Le Rêve

Kivoruty

Bobby Metz's Headache

Waiting for Katrina

Jim Bob

My Sister

Next Time, A Rabbit

The Road to Pyrus

Miracles

The Courier

Molly

LeRêve

You could set your watch by the thunderstorms that swept through the campus every August afternoon; dramatic clouds raced across the sky, accompanied by jaw-dropping lightning shows and rifle shots of thunder, then large, refreshing raindrops pelted down through heavenly shafts of sunlight, leaving a bright sheen on everything in sight, and that clean, bracing, ozone smell in the air. Three years earlier, the venerable east coast university that had conferred bachelor's and master's degrees on me had further extended my illusion of eternal youth by inviting me to join the faculty whilst I pursued a PhD. But on that final day of the summer quarter of 1978, after an otherwise jubilant sun shower, the sight of the historical buildings and eager co-eds that had once buoyed me with gratitude and vigor made me want to lock myself in an attic and read Kafka until I expired.

My teaching career had begun with great promise. I ignited my students' imaginations with what are now called multi-media lesson plans. I created new courses in literature, creative writing and psychology. My mind churned with ideas for my novel and fresh insights into my doctoral thesis. The administration had me on the fast track to tenure and, of course, I loved the attention. I was invited to every function on and off campus, and women practically lined up to offer themselves to me.

Three years later, after two close calls with professor/student regulations and a month in mandatory alcohol rehab, my creative desire was all but gone. I 'borrowed' lackluster lessons from old plans. I dozed off during oral recitations. I became the subject of idle, subtle ridicule. I locked the door to my office and stared out the window and the vibrant campus life around me while I dwelt on vague thoughts of suicide – lame, pathetic ideas like hiking myself to death or overdosing on niacin. My live-in girlfriend and fellow faculty member, Jane, who once inspired me to new intellectual and sexual heights, had begun to view my growing malaise as a contagious illness that might infect her. My sullen solipsism was sapping the energy out of our life together. Not even her orgasmic nipples, her show biz smile, or her continual craving for my body could keep my interest up. I hadn't touched her, or anyone else, for three months.

I was taken by surprise one very hungover Saturday morning when Jane informed me, out of the blue, that she'd accepted an offer to teach at a small, private liberal arts college in Big Sur. She confessed to a secret, life-long dream of living out west, tearfully admitting that this choice might spell the end of *us*, reminding me how much I loathed vegetables and getting up early. Her announcement broke through my pathetic self-absorption and knocked me speechless. I could hardly breathe, picturing my darling Jane sitting cross-legged on a beach, staring at the sunset and munching avocado wraps while discussing existential polytheism with some faux yogi named Brad. She cried and cried and swore she still loved me, all the while methodically packing her bags; her words whined like a trite, shallow love song you hear when your radio accidentally lands on a soft rock station. I clenched my teeth and wished her well, but I wanted to run down to the basement and cry. Another woman was leaving me, albeit for a very good reason, but who cares about facts and logic when you're being dumped. She was too kind to tell me to fuck off and die of self-pity. As she strode out the door towards the serenity of the Pacific Ocean, I had a minor epiphany. I was like the guy who drives drunk for years and doesn't realize what a fool he is until he has an accident and nearly kills himself. I suddenly saw my life not as I once hoped it would be or as I rationalized it might yet become. For the first time ever, I saw my life for what it was, and it was definitely time for a change.

My request for a year's sabbatical from the old-fart board of regents was granted immediately, indicating that Jane wasn't the only one on campus aware of my downward spiral. On the Tuesday after she left for the land of cliff houses and golf courses, I flew to Paris, hoping an extended stay in the world capital of art and artists would

jar my creative urges into gear, not to mention that anything
I might accomplish in France would look good on my
résumé. At the very least, I would be among thousands of
Parisians as cynical and annoying as I had become.

I found a cheap place in Montmartre and settled into
a rut immediately, sipping espresso at the same table and
mindlessly munching the same *jambon et fromage* baguette
for lunch every single day. I was too depressed to eat
dinner. I signed up for a course on Rimbaud but quit after
one class. I spoke to no one but waiters. I shuffled past
world famous museums and cathedrals, blithely unaware of
the classic beauty surrounding me. I liked going out, but not
for any specific reason other that my place felt cramped,
like most dwellings in Europe. A typical evening consisted
of nursing a beer alone in a corner of La Coupole, watching
from across the room as *avant-garde* filmmakers and
stunningly beautiful women amused one another.

I hadn't read one single book in Paris, even though
my sublet was miraculously lined with English titles. Nor
had I written a single word on the stack of writing tablets I
purchased upon my arrival. The few times I sat at the *belle
epoque* desk in my flat with pencil in hand, I was attacked
by thoughts of Jane and all the others before her who had

walked out on me, yet not a word of those intense emotions landed on paper. The closest I had come to being with a woman was a brief meeting with an Algerian who hoped to sell his teenage daughter to a wealthy Canadian (I often wore a Maple Leaf t-shirt to elicit better service). Months crept past my paralyzed brain.

As Christmas approached, my life was as void of direction as when I had arrived. I wandered the streets searching for signs of the holiday blues to keep my misery company. But Paris had no droll Santas listlessly ringing bells or shopping malls filled with angry bargain hunters—only millions of tiny cars racing in circles and an icy breeze that kept my nose perpetually runny. I felt recurrently suicidal as I watched folks from all over Europe shopping and toasting and snapping photos, the cafés even more crowded as the weather wedged everyone indoors.

One chilly Friday afternoon, unable to find the French word for noose in my conversational dictionary, I mechanically donned my long winter coat and descended into the underground infrastructure of the city. I hopped the first Métro train that came along, thinking perhaps I might purchase some heroin, or a pistol. The only thought in my meager brain was a fleeting hope that an angry Palestinian might take me hostage. I stared blankly at people's shoes in a state of absent-minded hostility. A fellow traveler, sitting too close to me as the French are prone to do, jerked his head around and briefly glared at my abdomen. My growling stomach had become louder than the train. I disembarked at the next station, one I did not recognize, and headed straight for a corner bistro, which happened to be called *Le Rêve*. I chuckled to myself, ruminating on the name. Did dreams come true for those who entered? Or was it named in honor of Picasso's erotic, fractured painting? What part of town was this anyway?

The patrons inside were no different from any other Parisian café: the wife and the husband, silently smoking, each in their own world; the shop girl with her young beau copping a feel under the table; the working lads revving up on cheap beers for a weekend of nightclubbing; a fashionable lady laden with shopping bags; and the ubiquitous, nostalgic pensioner, kvetching about the late President deGaulle to no one in particular. I thought I would warm myself with some brandy and a pastry, then maybe walk around this unknown part of town, perhaps search for some anti-American graffiti or a puppet show. I sat on a bench in a far corner, away from the chill of the doorway, unfolded a discarded copy of *Le Monde,* and treated myself to a Martel.

    I never saw her come in. She seemed to appear out of the cigarette haze that hung throughout the place. She sat alone against the wainscoting on the opposite side of the bistro, nursing a pink fizzy drink. Outside the window behind her, the sun sank and clouds thickened, matching her dark expression. At first, I thought she was waiting for someone as she looked up whenever the door opened. After a while it became clear that this mysterious, exotic woman was alone. *Le Rêve,* indeed.

    With the fall of darkness came rare December snowflakes. The proprietor prodded the fireplace to life as the clientele buzzed about the possibility of a *Noël Blanc.* I watched over the top of my newspaper as my *femme fatale* in the far corner nonchalantly slid her wool coat off her shoulders. Her dark blue silk blouse showed off her bare arms, which were slim and smooth. Her grey skirt seemed too short for the season, and her knee-high black leather boots tapped the floor nervously. A barely discernable slouch tainted her mien with sadness. She stared downward into her glass, only raising her eyes to request another Campari and soda.

She unfolded a wrinkled one-page letter with red and blue Airmail stripes around its edge. She read it several times, occasionally moving her lips, as though she were repeating a phrase to herself. I took her to be an artist longing for her absent lover. I imagined him composing the letter in a tropical Amazon rainforest or a snow-capped village in Bhutan where he was painting abstract canvases of tribal life. I heard myself think—now *there's* a story—my first creative thought in a year! I imagined she missed his smell, his arrogance. I wondered if *Le Rève* was their favorite spot, if Campari bitters his favorite drink. She lit a cigarette and continued to read and reread.

I envied her heartache. I wanted to pine for someone, to feel passion again. Her eyes narrowed as she reread the letter for the umpteenth time. Even though the hearth had warmed the room, a shiver shook her body. She slid her slim arms into the sleeves of her wool coat and clutched it snugly around her shoulders. I prayed she wasn't preparing to leave. I was already linked to her; she was my evening, my fantasy, my New Year's Resolution. I considered following her if she left. In America, a man could be arrested for that kind of behavior. In Europe it's called romance.

I asked the *garçon* to please inquire if the lady would care for another Campari and some company. He was forgiving of my accent, and seemed capable of getting my request right. When he interrupted her reverie and conveyed my suggestion, she burst into tears. Without looking my way, she stood up, jammed the letter in her pocket, and made for the door, banging her leg on the table and knocking over her drink. The waiter looked across the room at me and shrugged. I fished some francs from my pocket, waved them in the air for him to see, slipped them under my empty snifter and hurried after her.

I squinted up and down the deserted streets. My eyes adjusted to the darkness as large snowflakes melted on my lashes. A tomcat howled from a window. Little pops of light under distant streetlamps didn't help much. It was the click-clack of her shoe taps that turned my head. She had stopped under a shop awning at the other end of the block, clutching her coat under her chin as though it had no buttons. I wondered if she was giving me a chance to catch up. Maybe her leg that hit the table was throbbing, making it painful to walk. That collision was going to leave an ugly bruise. As I headed toward her, I saw her toss match after match aside, spitting out, "Ah!" after each failure to light her cigarette in the winter wind.

I joined her beneath the overhang, which offered no protection from the weather as the wind blew the snow horizontally. Without a word, she handed me the matchbox, turned toward me, and held the cig to her lips. Tears had streaked both her cheeks. She looked down, her lips quivering, her shoulders instinctively curved forward and up against the cold. I grabbed her arms, turned her back to the wind, and flipped her collar up. I then invoked my drugstore cowboy training: cupping my hands, striking the match, and immediately enclosing it in the little bowl made by my fingers. I noted a flicker of appreciation in her upward glance. That first, strong chestful of smoke seemed to save her life. She inhaled deeply twice more, then finally looked up and studied my face. Her eyes were hazel with yellow flecks, like tiny slivers of gold flake. I measured her look to be one of gratitude for following her, for making the effort. Just then, a police Peugeot hurtled down the narrow street toward us with its signature two-note siren, a red-eyed Cyclops in the otherwise black and white scene. She clutched my arm and stood perfectly still until the *gendarmes* had passed, then she tugged at me without a word, and steered us around the corner and away from the café.

As we walked through the wet snowflakes with our backs to the wind, my mind stepped back and watched us. I was in a noir film—my destiny uncertain, my heart leading me into an unfamiliar corner of a foreign city, at the mercy of a woman who had magnetically drawn me away from benign ambivalence and a warm brandy.

This had been a fantasy of mine since my first visit to Paris, when my teenage senses had been aroused by the stunning architecture and the ubiquitous smells of Gaulois smoke, diesel delivery trucks, and poodle shit. The jangling bustle of Frenchmen gesturing and talking *très rapidement* engaged my brain like music. I swooned for French women with their strong noses and lacy bras, exuding feminine confidence like proud flowers. Fifteen years later I was being led down a wet, cobbled street by an enigmatic stranger, the intermittent streetlamps accenting our cheekbones one moment and casting long shadows the next.

She stopped at an odd little house, smaller and older than its neighbors, as if the street had undergone a facelift and missed her building. Perhaps a favored relative of Baron Haussmann, the great 19th century urbanizer, had lived there during the fabled reconstruction of Paris and it escaped razing. She pressed her body against mine and tucked her head into my chest. I had been lured by her mystery, but my curiosity had since been replaced by desire. I imagined her skin on mine, freed from our swaddling layers of winter wool.

She turned toward the faded red door and tugged at my arm, inviting me inside and up a narrow stairway. An iron railing, also painted red, rose alongside the stairs, which were barely wide enough for the two of us. We left the cold behind as we climbed up, arriving at the third floor in front of a door too small for my height. She used a brass skeleton key from an empty flowerpot to let us in. I thought, why even bother locking it? She switched on a small lamp sitting on a table that took up unnecessary space in a room that could spare none—evidence of her choosing to please her senses rather than some spatial convention. Next to the lamp was a square, green vase supporting a handful of bright yellow plastic daffodils, one of the many splotches of color in an otherwise white apartment. A red oval rug colored the only open space in the wide board floor. The entire room was maybe ten by twenty feet, with a large dormer window in the slanted ceiling. The far wall contained a sink, stove, a pair of blue cabinets, and a mini fridge under a worn, unpainted counter. A drafting table with a tall metal stool stood in the dormer. The room was noticeably warm but I detected no source of heat. There was no bed.

She tossed her coat on a plastic side chair and put the kettle on. She came up behind me and slid my coat off, pointed me to a white muslin loveseat and tossed my coat on top of hers. Not a single word had passed between us. On the wall behind the couch hung a museum-framed oil painting of two women standing side by side, looking up at a cloudless blue sky. One face had dark brown eyes, the other hazel. The sky took up most of the painting. It might have been painted from a photograph and she was the hazel-eyed one. I didn't see any names on the mailbox downstairs, and there were only the initials, "C. J." on the painting. Colette? Camille? Something in me didn't care, didn't want to know the details. As a sailor friend once told me, when you're in over your head, it doesn't matter how deep it is.

She wordlessly prepared chamomile tea, its peaceful, outdoor aroma wafting through the small apartment. I watched her move about the place. Her body was narrow, but her back was broad and straight; her spine and ribs showed through her blouse when she bent to retrieve the tea tray. I imagined her wavy, chestnut hair would fall past her shoulders, but for tonight it was scrunched atop her head haphazardly, full of pins and clips, a perfect, stylish mess. She was one of those lucky people who rarely fret over appearances yet always manage to come off looking smart.

I felt calmed by the silence and aroused by observing her simple movements. I glanced around her narrow garret, estimating her life. The collection of furniture and objects was eclectic; nothing matched— everything looked second-hand and unique, including the worktable with the tilting top. She seemed too young, too elegant to be poor. She was certainly an artist, but not of the starving class. I suppose it would have been more relaxing if I had been able to just sit there—be in the moment, as they say—but I was very busy accumulating clues to her identity and working out our future together. I am invariably attracted to wiry, dark women in distress like a moth to cashmere. Jane said it was because they were easy to leave when the magic wore off. Jane's brand of honesty could be pretty harsh. She knew about my relations with

Monica and Shelly and Barbara: all three were artists, all quirky, passionate and needy, all gone in two months.

Jane was the first girl I had stuck with in a while. My friend Zack said she was a sign I was maturing, like he would know—my shameless, name-dropping friend who smoked tiny Dutch cigars because he'd seen William Hurt smoke them in a movie. Nevertheless, Jane was to me what oxygen is to a tired athlete; she revived my weary heart and drew me in without the allure of a dark past, without psychotic drama or bizarre sex. She was simply a good person. She grew up in Iowa, went to Michigan on scholarship, and taught high school while she studied for her Masters at Harvard to qualify for teaching at the college level. When we met, her ambition was simply to enjoy life and share her good fortune. She was the best thing that could happen to any man who wanted a normal life. It turned out that I was to her what Monica and the others were to me, a dark alley off the main street of life, where one might find a gem in the trash, but more likely danger and regrets.

Was my silent *Parisienne* with the golden-flecked eyes a further diversion from my returning to academia, earning a doctorate, and finishing my novel? She turned from the kitchen, carrying a tray with a hand painted ceramic teapot and two mismatched cups without saucers. I wondered if she made all these things herself? I swear the wooden tray could have been carved that morning. When she bent over to set the tray down on a small round table, the top of her blouse fell open. She was braless with small, firm, champagne glass breasts. The tray contained two cloth napkins, spoons, a sugar bowl, and a small ceramic pitcher of milk. For an American reluctantly accustomed to sitting on a stool at some faculty couple's kitchen island and helping himself to skim milk from the Amana, this scene was ethereal and cinematic. She finally joined me on the loveseat and poured our tea. As I lifted the cup to my lips and blew on the hot tea, she stretched out her legs, slowly unzipped her boots, and set them off to the side, out of sight. She wore low white cotton socks, like schoolgirls wear with Mary Janes. Her legs were lean and smooth. I had a feeling she would have put her legs up across mine were it not for the tea service.

She still hadn't spoken. The only sound was the delicate clink of her spoon. Aside from my instinct for mystery and my lust for this particular girl, I still wasn't quite sure what I was doing there. I remembered the letter.

Was I saving her from suicide? Was I the rebound man from the letter writer? She put her cup down, and for the first time since we stood together under the awning, she looked into my eyes. I set my cup down on the table and turned to meet her gaze. After a few seconds, both of us, almost imperceptibly, leaned forward.

I've always been fascinated by that magical instant when two people who do not know each other simultaneously decide to become lovers. It's a strange and complete transformation, from being dressed and having only recently met, to allowing a total stranger intimate access to one's naked body. Twenty minutes earlier we had been patrons of a café, like the pensioner or the shop girl. Then we were immutably entwined together on her sofa, bound by a tacit covenant to share the same space.

I relished our pungency in my nostrils, the sparkle in her eyes. Never mind the letter or her name or the tears in the café. I held her close and memorized the sensations as our breathing slowed. These delicious moments would be gone soon enough.

She began to cry quietly.

Oh, God. What now? She folded her arms across her chest, one hand covering each breast. She hunched forward, protecting her vulnerability.

"What's the matter?" I asked.

"*Rien. C'est normal. Pour moi.*"

Normal? With every guy? Every orgasm? The mood vanished. I hate crying. I wanted to leave. I hated France. I made a move to get up and she grabbed me like a life preserver. She held my arm tight with both hands and did that burrowing thing again, with her face in my neck, like a foal nuzzling its mother. I exhaled and allowed her in, softened by her warmth.

The door opened downstairs. I jumped like I had been poked in the ribs. I was certain it was her boyfriend returning from Tonga armed with a souvenir ceremonial machete. Frenchmen can be very emotional. She held me tight.

"*Non, non.*" She pointed to the floor, indicating (I hoped), that it was her neighbor. Maybe so, but I was jumpy. I needed to move around. Maybe a change of scenery. I wrested my arm from under her, stood up, and looked around for my clothes. She jumped off the couch, naked, and headed for the stove. "*Encore du thé?*" She relit the burner and turned to face me. I looked at her small, brown nipples, her little girl socks, the bruise on her thigh just above her knee. Her hair was falling out of its arrangement; ringlets and strands framed her face and caressed her neck and shoulders. I could not have imagined a sweeter, more erotic picture. I was powerless. She sealed the deal by offering me a robe she pulled from an open closet. It fit perfectly. I thought, if that guy shows up and sees me wearing his robe, he's definitely going to kill me. The good news was that he was my size, and not some Samoan rugby player. She found a red silk sheet on a chair and draped it loosely around herself.

She brought the tea and knelt on the other side of the low, three-legged table so she could look up at me. She offered me a Dunhill, and although I had quit when Jane left, I accepted. She lit us both with a Zippo, which told me why she couldn't light her smoke with matches in the wind. She was spoiled. And she liked American things.

"*Je ne parle pas bien Français.*"

"Is okay." She smiled for the first time. "I am good with the English."

The Dunhill made me lightheaded. She closed her eyes and breathed deeply. Through the skylight I could see snow swirling around the roof.

She jumped up suddenly, "*Est-ce que tu veux…*? Oh, sorry, um, would you prefer something to eat? Some bread and jam?"

I had forgotten all about food, the original reason I had entered Le Rêve. "That would be great. Yes. *Merci.*"

The only way to describe the scene at the other end of her cozy space is to say that she looked just right, doing her post-coital nurturing thing. In her red silk wrap, she was my Christmas gift. My mind drifted back a few minutes: she had felt so perfect, tangled beneath me, seizing the rapture, her feral eyes fixed on mine. As I watched her examine little jars at the other end of the room, my chest began to fill up with hope and anxiety.

We spent every night together until the following Easter. Neither of us ever mentioned the letter or the robe, and it turned out she was pretty 'good with the English.' Not that it mattered. We communicated on a silent, deeper level than I had ever felt, before or since. We held a wordless agreement between us, an extension of the one sealed with our eyes when I lit her cigarette under the awning in the snow. And I soon discovered that she did cry after every orgasm, which I grew to anticipate and relish. I rethought all my so-called beliefs about romantic love during the time I spent with Claire. Oh, yes, that was her name, Claire. Her mother, also a lover of drama, had named her after the actress, Claire Bloom.

My lone offer of work as an English tutor never came through and I ran out of money in April. I could have tried harder, but I didn't. Claire was living off a modest trust fund and earned spending money as an illustrator. I couldn't picture myself staying with her once my funds ran out. It's a guy thing. I was afraid of losing the confidence she adored. The dream was ending.

Something compelled me to return to the life that had shaped me, the world that was branded in my brain. As my students would say, "Whassup with that?" Don't ask me. But things worked out. It's a long story. Simply put, Jane grew weary of tofu and stunning scenery. She missed four seasons and the poetic irony of our unique union. We married shortly after her return and our fraternal twins graduated from Stanford and UCLA (talk about irony). I'll probably make Dean next year and Jane is still the sexiest woman on earth. She is currently working on a memoir of our family's journey and I feel lucky she still wants me.

Claire will always be at the top of my list of 'what ifs,' but I regret nothing. She had wanted me to stay on with her that April in Paris, but she understood what I needed to do, and didn't object or make a scene. Europeans have that knack for accepting life as it is. On my first trip back there a few years later for a seminar on semantics, I sought out the neighborhood where we met and lived together for four months, but I couldn't find it. There was no Le Rêve in the phone book. I briefly considered the existence of an alternate universe, but I chose to stow those memories, and flew home to New England.

Jane and I spend three weeks in Wiscasset, Maine every summer and the twins and their families visit from California at Christmas. They complain about the cold weather but at least they're not vegetarians.

Kivoruty

Kivoruty stood perfectly at attention in formation, his eyes forward, his mandibles aligned, his feelers proudly presented, in the front rank of his platoon of red army fire ants as the ant Bishop and the ant President for Life paraded past, observing the polished feelers and devout postures of the red army fire ants, and inspecting the ceremonial piles of wood chips and peony petals they had gathered for the celebration. In the hazy distance, the Queen Ant observed the ritual from a shaded pavilion of cottonwood leaves, surrounded by scores of her attendants. The columns and

ranks of the ant brigade stood honored in respect for Her
Majesty, beaming with intense pride in their unity and
oneness, their singular devotion to the Queen. Their
thoraxes puffed with distinction, having succeeded through
primary ant school, military camps and advanced moral ant
training seminars, where Kivoruty and his comrades had
been ritually instructed in the instinctive yet advanced ways
of adult male anthood, which consisted of two primary
duties: the protection through violent force and the dutiful
sexual worship of Her Highness.

Kivoruty hoped for special distinction that day,
despite being lined up directly next to his nemesis, the
ambitious and inordinately handsome Malcovni, whose
thorax boasted etchings and other honors bestowed upon
him during his hugely successful initiation and advanced
training period. Malcovni was bigger than Kivoruty, and
stronger and better looking. He had been destined since
pupa phase toward red army ant renown and he knew it. He
fully expected to be first in line to inseminate Her
Highness, an honor reserved for the single most outstanding
ant in the colony. Kivoruty stood tall nonetheless, feeling
fortunate to be in the front ranks during the inspection
where he would be able to see the Queen, and where the

Bishop and the President for Life might notice his spectacular feelers and mandibles. He had been aware since his pupa stage that he was a runt in the feeler department, and the only way he was ever going to copulate with the Queen, was to find to a way to stand out from his fellow red army ants. He'd spent several hours before the inspection working on his diminutive, yet super-sensitive feelers, polishing them to an ultra-high sheen and exercising their sensitivity. Unfortunately for Kivoruty, being positioned next to the much-admired Malcovni, made it practically impossible for anyone to even notice the results of his labor and devotion.

But when the parade passed by their position, for some miraculous, unknown reason, the President for Life and the Bishop both stopped in their tracks at the same instant. Kivoruty naturally assumed they were taken by the magnificent *formicidae* specimen standing next to him. Their twelve legs stopped moving at once, but their compound eyes were not focused on Malcovni. No, the two ant colony nabobs did not stop to acknowledge the prize red army ant that his comrades admired and envied. They were entranced by and drawn to the gleaming, perfectly shaped *antennae* on Corporal Kivoruty. They came closer and inspected his feelers with utmost curiosity. It didn't take long for them to agree that Kivoruty should be singled out at once, not only for the highly polished condition of his feelers, but also for the spectacular physical condition of his three-part body and the eager attitude which shone from his eyes. Before the disbelieving eyes of the great Malcovni and every ant in the formation, The President for Life and The Bishop broke with tradition, and Kivoruty was given the exalted privilege of being the first army ant to have sexual intercourse with the Queen the following morning.

The Queen red fire ant was The Treasured Supreme Ruler of All, including the President for Life and all the other higher ups. To mate with her was the ultimate life dream of every single red army ant. Kivoruty had achieved this goal despite his limited gifts, filling him with joy, but also making him quite anxious and unable to sleep at all during the night. He wisely spent those sleepless hours preparing himself psychologically for the mounting of Her Highness and the next morning he walked erect, striding out of the barracks past the envious eyes of his fellow soldier ants. When The Queen personally opened the flower petal door of her chambers and extended her royal feelers out in the direction of our hero, Kivoruty broke ranks and marched proudly towards the Royal Abode.

Unfortunately for Kivoruty and The Queen, and every other ant in the colony, a ten-year-old girl's mountain bike bounced off a nearby woodsy trail at that crucial moment, its tire squashing Her Highness to bits and throwing the entire colony into mayhem and anarchy. An ant colony without a Queen, by definition, is no longer a colony. There was nothing in the DNA of red army ants to guide them in a life without their Queen. Suddenly, everything they had been taught or knew instinctively was erased in an instant when the girl's tire crushed the Queen into crackly smithereens. Kivoruty stood in stunned silence at the sight of the bloody destruction mere centimeters from his eyes. The goal of his entire existence, the ultimate climax of all his training and hope was erased in a nanosecond. The horror of the sight of her mangled body threw Kivoruty into a state of emotional devastation and despair never before known among this simple creature.

The ranks of soldier ants ran amok, scattering their number all over the place like headless chickens, like earthworms splayed in a hundred directions by floodwaters. Some ran quickly to The Water Source to commit insecticide while others marched blindly behind their brother ants in front of them who didn't know where they were going either. No one knew what to do in a world without a Queen. Every single surviving red army ant had the same thought, he would have preferred that bicycle tire to have taken his life rather than endure an empty, pointless, Queen-less existence.

No such luck for poor Kivoruty, whose entire life had consisted of preparation for performing sex with his Queen. He was doomed to survive and wander aimlessly for the rest of his life, his entire body in a permanent state of arousal. He wanted to die, but clean drinking water and heavenly morsels to eat seemed to magically appear before him. For any other species, this would have been the luckiest streak one could hope for, but for a red army ant without a Queen, Kivoruty's bountiful path was hell on earth. A random, hideous mocking by the universe continued to shine unwanted good fortune on him, extending his life longer than any red army ant in the history of their kind. He would have preferred to have his appendages ruthlessly yanked out one at a time by a kindergarten boy or to have his multi-faceted eyes poked blind by a million nanoshards of smashed fluorescent tubing. He hoped he might accidentally stumble onto a lump of super glue in a tool shed and remain fixed to the spot while an open can of varnish spontaneously combusted, causing the shed to burn to the ground and turning Kivoruty into an Asian appetizer. But no such merciful end was in the cards for the loyal, hopeful corporal; he was forced to survive, to continue marching forward with no destination and no hope, doomed to endure his seemingly endless remaining days in a world without a Queen. From an ant's point of view, this existential torture, this meaningless existence, this Kafka-esque scenario seemed to go on forever - but not really. Kivoruty's entire life span was only a few weeks.

Bobby Metz's Headache

My career is going well. People want to know me.
Women are hitting on me. So why am I complaining to my
one and only friend? My middle-aged, white friend, Dennis,
who, in an embarrassing attempt to retrieve someone else's
youth, has given himself the 'street name' of DizzyD. He's
the only friend I had before I got famous who's still alive,
and he's taken an hour off from his limo driving job to sit
across from me in some upper west side, gluten-free,

hipster internet place, so I can bend his ear about my persistent, pervasive depression. I don't really expect him to get it, and he proves me right by making lame suggestions like, "You should try one of them day spas. They got cute chicks and Jacuzzis and shit." As he yada yadas on about his last massage, an image of my father flashes into my head.

Whenever my Pops heard anybody talking about modern solutions to stress, he always said, 'I must've got off the bus at the wrong stop.' Pops hated to hear anyone complain. His entire generation was never in pain and never asked anyone for help. He worked construction for forty years, never made foreman, and dropped dead on the job. He tried to pass his toughness down to me. When I was little and tripped on the sidewalk, my mother reached down to help me, and he barked, 'Don't! You're gonna spoil the kid.' He didn't make me tough, he made me mad. He made us all mad. My mother hated the patriarchal system that made him the boss, my father hated her for controlling his sex life, and I hated them both for making me think about all this crap. All I wanted to do was bury my face in my mother's massive, cushiony breasts where my father and school and every other crummy annoyance in the borough of Queens went away.

I have been chasing that feeling ever since I can remember. I'm a short, hairy guy with mediocre looks and *savoir faire* to match, but when I buried myself in a woman, the world went away and I felt like I was gonna be happy forever. I spent my twenties and thirties lusting from one female body to another. As my youth receded further into the past, fewer and fewer women were buying my act. I developed headaches and my ankles started to hurt to the point where I had to give up neighborhood handball. I ate Motrin for the pain. Doctors couldn't find anything wrong with me. I complained a lot. The people I had called friends fell away one by one. Dennis suggested I take up poker. For once, I took his advice, but after a year and a half and several costly excursions to Atlantic City, I gave that up, too.

The worst part about my downward, backward slide was that the occasional one-night-stand no longer distracted me from the anguish of my loneliness. I tried hookers. They were very sweet, which surprised me, and of course the sex was technically superior, but there was no love. I know it sounds stupid to expect love from a whore, but I couldn't help it. I've been looking for that feeling you're supposed to get from real love since forever, but good sex was as close as I ever came. For the first time in my life, I slipped into a state of self-pity. Deep inside I realized that no amount of fornication or televised sports or Jack Daniels was ever going to make me feel like a regular person, whatever that is. I was disgusted with myself and I didn't know what to do about it.

It took an accidental fling with crime to turn my fortunes around. I was cajoled into abetting a burglary, and I, the smartest guy on the job by half, was the only one who got caught. Things turned out okay for me, however. I ended up doing a nickel at Attica because I wouldn't rat out my buddy Nitro, rest his soul, and while I was there I taught myself to write. They had a pretty decent library and it didn't take long to figure out that the screws gave special treatment to peaceable inmates who posed no threat to the prison structure. Add to that the do-gooder philanthropists and bleeding-heart editors (all females) who wanted to help rehabilitate us felons, albeit for their own aggrandizement, which was fine with me. In short, my time in stir wasn't so bad. While the rest of the jailbirds were diddling their cellmates and writing pornographic love letters to chicks

who sent them sexy pictures, I latched on to middle-aged
women with a penchant for literature.

I learned fast. I composed violent, brutal poems. I
wrote flash fiction in the second person. My grisly, graphic
stories glamorized *life on the inside*. Park Avenue broads
loved the power of my voice and couldn't wait to promote
me. They loved to get their emotional hands dirty a few
minutes a month, so long as their marble sinks and soap
rosettes were only a limo ride away. Then there was the
exceptional, committed Mrs. Markham, who made the trek
upstate several times. She looked pretty good sitting across
the metal table in the visitor's room with the guard standing
right outside the bars listening to everything we said. She
wore low cut silk blouses under Chanel suits and kept
crossing and re-crossing her legs the whole time. She
gushed and she flirted. She quoted my poems *verbatim* and
promised me powerful connections. She was the one who
advised me that memoirs were all the rage as she sat there
squirming in her seat, gawking at my biceps and hairy
chest. Talk about working the system. A blind idiot could
have pulled off what I did.

When I was paroled, I didn't have to go looking for
a job with a criminal record hanging over my head like the

other stiffs, because, thanks to Mrs. Markham, *et al*, I had been published! My first memoir was flying off the shelves. Precious, artsy journals were begging me for material. I had a three-book deal at Knopf. *Vanity Fair* won the bidding war to serialize the first chapters of my next work. I was invited to every A-list event. People were dying to glimpse me in the flesh so they could feel better about the world they wanted to believe in, a world where hardened criminals could become fruitful members of society, a world where the misfortunate could be restored to a useful place by philanthropic matrons, a world where art is more important than true understanding.

When Oprah called, I told my agent to put on the brakes. Don't get me wrong, I love the attention, and my public life was great for sales, but I consider myself a serious writer and I was spending more time having my picture taken than I was writing. To Dennis, however, my shallow life appeared to be an abundance of pleasure and satisfaction. His simple, immature dreams could be brought to fruition in a snap by my circumstances.

"Jesus, man, you go to openings and shit with celebrities, chicks are hitting on you all the time, and you got money in the bank. What's the fucking problem?"

Dennis is truly a good guy and would definitely come through in a pinch if I ever needed a last-minute limo to JFK, but he's mentally stuck back in Rego Park, and he'll always be leaning on a parking meter as far as I'm concerned. Still, he's my only friend from the old days and therefore, the one person who's truly being honest with me at all times. So, I pick up the check and he's my sounding board, my connection to my roots, to reality, to the truth. He was the only friend who showed up at Pops' funeral, and he didn't bug me or try to make me feel better. I loved him for letting me grieve in my own way.

Mom did not cry one drop that day. I guess she loved Pops the way married people did back in the day, but when he died, she was finally free to pursue her decades-long dream—a modern, successful man who couldn't keep his hands off her. Turns out she had been stashing dough in the back of the maple armoire in the foyer and made some secret investments in beach property down in Neponset, which were now worth a fortune. Between that and the old man's life insurance, she was set.

We are definitely a family of transformation, with both my mother and I turning life-long resentments into late-blooming success. First I go from being an accidental convict to a *cause célèbre*, then my mom morphs from the bitter housewife into the rich widow, shopping at Bergdorf's and sipping midnight cocktails at the Carlyle. You'd think we'd run into each other in the moneyed part of town, but mom doesn't want to have anything to do with me. She sees me as just another jerk who got caught, like some stranger in a newspaper story. She doesn't deserve the title of mother. You'd think after what we'd both been through, she'd at least return my calls. Well, she can go fuck herself. I'm not wasting any more energy on her. She'll die soon enough and be out of my hair. That's what happens in families. Hey, I didn't invent this world. I'm just making my way in it.

All this reflective reminiscence takes place behind my sunglasses as I listen to the personal opinions of Dennis/DizzyD, whose idea of a big thrill is sniffing the back seat of his limo after driving Maria Sharapova over to Teterboro. Yet he's the only person on earth I can trust to give me an honest answer, albeit from a brain with an I.Q. of about 92. I drift back into the present, where I once again attempt to explain the pain of writer's block and listen to Dennis's diversion therapy suggestions.

"Hey, man," he says, leaning forward in his eagerness to get through to me, "Look at the bright side. You could be Nitro. At least you're alive."

I think back on the horrible hit-and-run driver that ended the life of our other friend, my former partner in crime, and I kinda see his point. Kinda.

"That's one way of looking at things, I suppose, but it's not enough."

He stares at me, incredulous.

"What's the matter with you, Bobby? Don't you *want* to be happy?"

Ouch, man. Finally, he said something that knocked on my door, but I wasn't in the mood to go there. Some other time.

"C'mon man, you know what I mean. It's too simplistic. I can't feel better just because I'm not dead."

Dennis continues to talk and I go in and out of daydreaming again. Thank God for sunglasses. My head is throbbing. This time my mind recalls, as it does too often, the tall, strawberry blond Julie Sykes, the girl with the cushiony breasts that I was crazy about in high school. The girl who looked straight through me because I was a short, dark, hairy guy that didn't play sports. I showed her, didn't I? Now I am a short, dark, hairy bestselling author.

What Julie Sykes probably didn't know, and what Dennis definitely doesn't know, and what no one else will ever know as long as I am alive is what happened on Senior Night at the Broadway Dance Hall in Manhattan when I did about a pound of cocaine. The entire senior class, drunk and stoned and terrified of the empty future most of us faced, were dancing to the music like it was their last night on earth. I kept going back and forth to the men's room, up and down the iron stairs, pissing out those Ballantine Ales, stuffing magic powder up my nostrils, and speaking to no one. I was staring at the distant Julie Sykes, the girl I had lusted after for all four years of my outcast high school life, the queen of our class, with an unbelievable body and an angel's face. My eyes followed her like a sniper as she danced with her boyfriend, drinking and laughing with her stuck-up friends whose guts I hated, her unassuming, natural beauty pulling my gaze to her like gravity.

Every source of light in the huge hall seemed to find her pearly-satin, strapless gown with a slit halfway up the skirt. Dazzling beams bounced off her diamond earrings, her blond hair grazed her bare shoulders. Her cleavage glistened from perspiration and the swirling disco ball. I sat on the same bar stool all night in a hyped-up, bleary-eyed state, expanding my fantasies as I ogled her from a distance between countless beers and trips to the john.

At one point, I stumbled out of the toilet and saw the untouchable Miss Julie, weaving up the stairs, wobbling on her high heels, heading for the ladies' room. She didn't even notice me in the doorway of the men's room, where I froze when I spotted her. She had a way of not even seeing people who weren't in her league. I couldn't take my eyes off her naked shoulders and her leg sliding in and out of that slit. When she walked unsteadily past me, I whiffed her famous gardenia perfume that had intoxicated me with resentment for four years. As she approached the door of the rest room, I was already in motion. I grabbed her arms and shoved her further down the hall and around a dark corner, smothering her body with mine, stifling her protests with my thick, angry hand. We were far from the dance floor and in total darkness. I wouldn't have cared where we were. I shoved my hand into that slit and tore at her lace undergarments. I opened her with my knees and forced myself into her as she bit my hand. She never stopped fighting. I kept going at her and going at her, but I couldn't get off. The lights swirled and flashed in the distance, the deafening disco music blasting from a thousand speakers. I bucked and pushed, stifling her screams with my hand, pounding her against the wall, my hips cramping and my legs wobbly. My body spasmed like an electric shock when I finally exploded inside her. I jerked my head back and screamed at the ceiling like a bloodthirsty, insane wolfman. Nobody heard me over the din of the music. Julie gave my hand one big chomp and twisted free of my grasp. I reeled backwards, losing my footing as everything around me spun wildly in circles. She ran for the stairs. I caromed off the railing, lurched toward the bathroom door, and stumbled to the floor. I was propped on my hands and knees, puking my guts up and probably ten seconds from a heart attack. I heard Julie's sobs dopplering away as I wretched, the sound of her heels clacking down the metal steps. I don't know how long I knelt there before I found the strength to get to my feet and stagger back downstairs. I never saw her again.

The following morning, as my musketeers tried to recall that night of all nights, Nitro mentioned that Julie Sykes seemed to have disappeared at some point. Dennis said she probably rode off into the sunset with Mr. Most Likely, Steve Lucas, in his Corvette, which everyone knew was purchased by his father's plumbing business. I'd bet money we all had the same image in our heads, of her round, tight ass ensconced in a leather bucket seat, further reminding us losers what we'd never have.

The smart guy that I think I am should have had a morning after epiphany at that moment, but I didn't. Intelligence, it turns out, has nothing at all to do with emotional or spiritual wisdom. I needed some time, some separation from the world, and, as it happened, several years behind bars to see things more clearly. People say things happen for a reason. I say people make up reasons for what happens because it drives them nuts when they don't understand stuff. If something doesn't follow logic they don't want to believe it. They call it a miracle, or an omen, or Murphy's Law. People don't know shit. They called it miraculous when a street corner kid from Queens arrived with the fucking *literati*, but the truth is, anything can happen and it often does. If only they knew.

In the midst of Dennis waning philosophical about women and money, I had an urge. I swiped my credit card at one of the computer stations and Googled the site that can trace anyone anywhere, and one more card swipe later, there she was, Julie Sykes, Ph.D., teaching graduate English at Columbia with the same last name, which could mean anything. I turned down Dennis's offer of a ride, promised him I'd call later, and hopped a cab up Broadway to 116th Street without a plan.

It's amazing how quickly you can find out whatever you want these days. One minute I get the notion to look up a girl I had tried not to think about every day for over twenty years, and a half hour later I am standing outside her classroom in Morningside Heights. The first thing I noticed through the beveled glass in the door was that the haunting face of Professor Sykes seemed almost as young and elegant as I remembered it from long ago. She was wearing tan corduroy slacks with wide pleats and a tailored, peach colored linen blouse that flattered her figure without drawing attention to it. A soft, coffee brown sweater was draped over shoulders. Her teal-rimmed glasses hung from a plain, black cord around her neck and balanced themselves directly above her memorable bosom. She stood almost perfectly still and as she lectured, her erect posture giving her the look of a gorgeous but old-fashioned school marm. I was mesmerized.

I flashed back to our high school cafeteria and recalled feeling overwhelmed with desire and envy by the simple sight of Julie Sykes eating lemon meringue pie. Still another flashback remained buried under consciously constructed layers of shame. The throbbing returned on both sides of my head, just above my ears. Now what? She didn't know I was there, and it wasn't incumbent upon me to let her know I was. God would have wanted me to do that but I hadn't listened to Him since my arrest. Then I thought, what the hell, I don't even know why I came up here. What if she sees me and suddenly remembers everything? What if she calls the cops? I know there's a statute of limitations on rape, but I'm still on parole. I don't know where I stand, legally. What the hell. Whatever force propelled my impulsive trip uptown was still there, demanding I see it through. I decided to find out how Julie Sykes got to where she is from where I left her.

While I waited in the hallway, I checked out the walls lined with portraits of old-boy types who personified the history of the English department and I reminisced about the history of my own life; which parts would make good fiction, which might spice up my second memoir and which parts were too dull to be revealed for any purpose. The raw pain above my ears was getting worse. I had a sudden hunch it might be related to why I was nabbed at the robbery years ago, and, for that matter, why I was creatively blocked today. It's no wonder everyone wants to fabricate memoirs - real life is too fucking unbelievable. Every time somebody tells me a true story that happened to them, it occurs to me that their tale would be rejected out of hand if it was pitched as fiction. Yet thousands of absurd events, impossible coincidences, hideous cruelties, and miracle outcomes occur every day. For example, who would believe that Julie Sykes of Rego Park, Queens, had been raped, did God knows what after that with or without Steve Lucas, then earned a Ph.D. and is teaching postgraduate English at Columbia? I was more than curious. I stood there in the empty hallway, jittering inside like a charged ion, waiting for a woman I hadn't seen for twenty plus years whom fate and an impulse had dealt back into my hands.

Never having been to college, I was expecting a bell to ring, so I was jarred out of my self-absorbed reverie when several doors opened and the fresh young faces of the future filed past me. As I made up stories about each one who walked by, taking casual note of some of the finest breasts in The Big Apple, I heard a refined, confidant female voice behind me. "May I help you?" I turned to face

Ms. Sykes, who was looking directly into my eyes and not recognizing me. She stood tall, her head several inches above mine. She carried a Coach messenger bag over her shoulder, and her face did not divulge a hint of emotion. She was merely offering to help a stranger find his way. She was apparently one of those rare people who seemed to view their circumstances without judgment or irony. I was disarmed. Why the hell did I come up here?

"Hi. It's me, Bob. Robert. Robert Metz? We went to high school together."

She looked a little closer with a slight squint, like someone trying to pick out a perp from a police lineup. My right eyebrow raised a few millimeters. *Does she remember?* She blinked and spoke. "Oh, uh, sorry. You look just like that fellow on the prison book."

"Yeah, that's me. And I'm also the guy you went to high school with twenty-two years ago. Remember? Bobby? We were in Mrs. Laughlin's English class together?"

She shook her head apologetically. "Really? I'm sorry. That was so long ago."

That nagging urge to reveal more was pushing its way forward in my consciousness, pressing against my skull, but I kept the lid on my emotions, continued to ignore my headache, and waited for her to remember.

"Remember, you sat in the front row?"

"Yes, I do remember. I sat there so I could make a good impression on Mrs. Laughlin."

I smiled, covering the lust and shame battling for control of my heart and mind. I recalled how great her ass looked from the back row in those snug, gray skirts that outlined her perfect figure. "No wonder you didn't see me. I was in the back."

"I'm sorry. Please don't think me rude."

"No problem." I made a mental note to spend more time with people who felt good about themselves and treated others with decency.

"Ohmygosh! Did you say you *were* that fellow who wrote the prison memoir?"

"Yep. That's me."

"Well, congratulations to you, Robert. Wow. That is not your average best seller, it's a very well-crafted, honest, intelligent piece of writing."

I blushed. My face hadn't colored like that since my only high school girlfriend, Angie (Don't call me Acne) Coluzzo, broke up with me in broad daylight in Taylor's

Pool Hall in front of everyone who mattered in my life at the time. That was the closest I ever came to intentionally committing a crime while sober.

"Thanks. It means a lot coming from an English professor." I felt a little confidence returning. Her face changed. She tilted her head and looked me over once more, this time with what felt like respect tinted with curiosity. A flicker of a smile curved the corners of her mouth. I felt emboldened. "Would you like to have a cup of coffee or something?"

She looked at me for a few more seconds without speaking. I could feel the discomfort of guilt pumping blood to my ears. "Ohmygosh! I am so sorry, but I have to teach another class in…" She shot her arm out of the sleeve of her cashmere sweater and looked at her gold watch. "…Two minutes, and it's all the way across campus. We can walk and talk, if you don't mind."

"Sure. Let's go." As she led the way, I snatched a peek at her left hand gripping the strap of her bag. No wedding ring. No jewelry at all. And where does a teacher get the dough to deck herself in cashmere and a Cartier watch? Maybe it was a gift from a rich boyfriend. Maybe it's a knock off from the Nigerians on Sixth Avenue.

Whatever. There was a lot to learn about Julie Sykes, but for now I was having trouble keeping up with her. So much for walking and talking. She was striding across campus like some kind of show horse. This was one of those people who gets things done. She suddenly stopped and looked at me as if I was someone else completely.

"I just had a great idea. My next group is Creative Non-Fiction, and I would love to have them hear it straight from the horse's mouth. What do you say?"

"I… I don't know. I mean, all I did was tell the truth in the book and…it kinda wrote itself, you know what I mean? Besides, I'm not exactly proud of what I did."

"Robert, don't be so modest. The bottom line here is that you're a bestselling author of a literate, emotionally daring memoir, and anything you say has 'street cred' with these kids, you know what I mean?"

Given my dark secret, it was the least I could do. "I suppose. Are you sure?"

"Yes, I'm sure. What have you got to lose? C'mon, it might be fun." She took off, not waiting for an answer.

I realized I was even more attracted (if that's possible) to the grown up version of the snob from high school, the victim from the dark hallway. I glimpsed a future where my luck was changing and I wouldn't need Dennis's retarded input to relieve my pain anymore. My instincts were driving me to seek female companionship to fill the nagging emptiness that lately had been striking me dumb at the keyboard. I doubled my steps to catch up with her.

She skipped up the steps to her building three at a time and yanked open the door for us. She grabbed my hand to guide me to the left down a hallway to the second door on the right, and into a classroom filled with a group of young people I would describe as smart-looking, whatever that means, and definitely eclectic – they were the human equivalent of the sampler platter at Spiro-The-Greek's in Flushing. I stared empty-eyed at the students, momentarily distracted by the thrilling, erotic sensation of Julie's hand briefly holding mine in the hallway.

"Good afternoon, everyone." The conversations stopped quickly as the students mumbled greetings to Ms. Sykes while giving me the once over. "We are in for a special treat today. We are going to spend half our time, or longer if he is willing, in a Q and A session with none other that the author of a best-selling example of creative non-fiction, which I believe is currently on the Times' list…"

"Forty-nine weeks." I didn't realize I had spoken. I blushed again.

"For forty-nine weeks. Not bad, huh, class? Well, then, let's get to it. Before we start, let me remind you to couch your criticisms into questions as you would with your classmates in a workshop situation, with an eye toward sharpening your own skills and, of course, with respect." She looked around the room as her instructions sank into the now alert brains. "Ladies and gentlemen, Mr. Robert Metz, author of "Not A Fish." The class applauded. Group behavior is funny, isn't it? People just do things they think they're supposed to do. Julie wasn't finished. "I have a question, Mr. Metz. Would you please tell the class where the title came from?"

The hand of an exceptionally pretty blonde in the front row shot up. "I know!"

Julie was still in charge. "Ms. Carlsson?"

"I read your book almost a year ago, and I totally loved it. I remember that because I wondered what the title had to do with the story. 'Fish' is prison jargon for new prisoners, right?"

It pained me to look at this Carlsson chick. She was the short, dark, hairy guy's wet dream; shoulder length, flaxen hair, perfect teeth, bright, blue-grey eyes, flawless skin that looked slightly tanned even in winter, large breasts and shapely calves, all clad in a short tweed skirt, a lime colored cotton sweater, and, get this, Keds!

"You're right. Ms. Carlsson, is it? That is where I got the title. I heard that expression after I'd been inside a few months, after a couple more shipments of 'fish' had arrived behind me. It gave me some perspective on what I was in for, and I had a kind of epiphany – you guys know what that means, right?"

I smirked as a titter of laughter rippled across the room.

"That day in prison I had what some call 'a moment of clarity.' It was the first time in my life I saw reality for what it was and I made a conscious decision to make it work *for* me instead of against me."

They were sitting there, every single one, staring at me in silent respect as if I was the fucking Dalai Lama. Unbelievable.

"The words 'not a fish' also relate to me feeling unlike the other cons - like a fish out of water, so to speak. Oh, and my publisher thought it was 'catchy.'"

More laughter. I loved it.

Julie chimed in, "Does anyone else have a question for Mr. Metz?" Every hand in the room went up. I swear it gave me a boner. Or maybe it was Blondie in the front row. It's hard to tell which was more of a turn on, swarms of anonymous literature worshippers wanting a piece of my mind, the girl of my dreams (and nightmares) from high school, or the glistening, elegant legs of Miss Norway. Some things never change.

The rest of the class flew by. I answered questions for the entire fifty minutes and then some. These MFA kids were smart. I probably learned a thing or three. There was no class scheduled in that room after us, so half the kids stayed and we kept the Socratic thing cooking until Julie smoothly interceded to close the session. When the last student had shaken my hand and left, hopefully on their way to Barnes & Noble to contribute to my next royalty check, Julie asked me if I still wanted that cup of coffee. "And it's on me. You've done me a huge favor today." If only she knew. I caught myself wondering what kind of panties she might be wearing. My boldness was expanding.

"Actually, I've built up an appetite. How about a late lunch or early dinner? It looks like you're done for the day."

"Very observant, my old friend. Like what you said about seeing reality without emotional lenses clouding your perception. Great point, and beautifully phrased."

"Can we stop talking about writing for while? I'd like to hear about you."

She smiled a humble, you-got-me smile and said, "Of course." She flipped open her cell phone. "Let me just call my daughter. She's coming home on her first holiday from grad school and she'll be expecting me."

My brain froze like I had been force fed nine Italian ices through my nose. Julie Sykes had a child. In grad school. I couldn't help doing the arithmetic.

She kept walking on ahead as she left the message for her daughter while I stood pinned to the floor. She stopped and turned back toward me, her curves silhouetted by the light from the double doors, her prize-winning smile lighting up the corridor.

"C'mon," she said, "What are you waiting for? Let's eat."

I looked at her eager, open expression and w⌐ what contorted shape her lovely face would t⌐' knew what I knew. It makes you won⌐ of truth is. My double-sided headache engulf my entire skull. My vision was fractured by a kaleidoscope of tiny shards of light caroming inside my eyeballs like shooting stars. Pain stabbed my ankles.

Up ahead, Julie looked back at me, tilting her head slightly to one side, as if she had come upon a lost child. "Are you all right?"

I stood frozen in place, silent.

Waiting For Katrina

It is August 18, 1968. I've been wandering through
Europe for seven weeks now, soaking up all the sights of
this historic continent that I'd only seen in books before; a
lifetime dream come true, that's for sure. But today is
different. I am stuck here, sitting on the edge of the lumpy
leather sofa of my budget *pensione* just off the baroque
main square in Old Town Prague. My eyes anxiously scan
the crowds as they traipse past the front window. I am

waiting for Katrina. The city is alive with the joyful celebration of a perfect summer day, sunny and warm, fueled by Alexander Dubcek's political reforms that have liberated Czechoslovakia from the oppressive control of the Soviet Union. Everybody's in a good mood. Songs blare from dozens of Sony Watchmen passing by. Thousands of tourists and students from all over the world have joined the Czechs to celebrate their new-found freedoms, but I am not dancing with them today. I am indoors, alone, waiting for Katrina.

We met at a crowded café just down the street from the Palace Hotel. She was talking and laughing with a big bunch of friends while I was frugally nursing a beer at the counter. Our eyes met and something happened. The noise of the café seemed to vanish and we were suddenly at a table for two and couldn't stop talking as we stared into each other's eyes. If only I'd been brave enough to admit my meager financial state to her that afternoon, I would probably have enough coin left over to court her for another week or two. But, alas, I was coaxed into a five star dinner on our first date. It's not her fault. A stunning, high-class beauty can't help having a taste for claret and taxicabs, and this naïve New Hampshire lad on his first jaunt overseas didn't know any better. I was swept away by her golden tresses and her broad, peaceful face with its curious, flecked blue eyes. Being with Katrina was like holding hands with a dream.

She agreed to meet me here at 2 o'clock, after lunch with her father, some big shot in the new government. What a life she has. She is beautiful, lively and smart. She wears colorful sundresses and silver ballet slippers. She speaks fluent English with a really cool accent. She is always in motion, the center of attention wherever she goes. I have no idea what she sees in me.

The high-ceiling lobby of my tiny hotel reeks of strong coffee, cigarettes and ammonia. Its stone floor has been worn smooth by thousands of feet over a hundred years. The only other piece of furniture in the reception area is a heavy, round, low table with three claw legs, decorated by a lone milk glass vase sporting five fresh red carnations and strewn with fashion and news magazines in Czech and French. I am not interested in magazines or anything else, for that matter. My eyes are glued to the street outside the window.

Katrina is late and doubts are growing in my heart and mind. I watch the throngs of happy people surge through the streets, dancing with strangers, spilling beer on one another, and frequently erupting in cheers for no apparent reason, in contrast to the anxious self-doubt eroding my confidence. My searching, squinting eyes are intermittently stung by bolts of sun-glare flashing off the windows of passing Opels and Peugots. Somewhere further down the lane, the lively whine of a concertina slices through the din of crowd noise.

Across the lobby, oblivious to the merry mobs outside, sits Marek, the *pensione* manager, perched on a high stool behind his counter, chain-smoking Marlboros and staring blankly at a small black and white television where a government spokesman is outlining further liberal reforms. Marek is Polish, about thirty, fair and slim with the beginnings of a beer belly. He and his pregnant wife Gosia live in a tiny flat at the rear of the ground floor. He loves his adopted city with a provincial passion common to those who've never been anywhere else, and will talk about it endlessly with the slightest provocation. I choose not to engage him even though it would help pass the time. The Bavarian cuckoo clock on the lobby wall sings out, "*Drei.*"

Prague in 1968 is the perfect party place for a college grad on summer vacation, and meeting Katrina was,

I thought, the icing on that cake. The problem is, I've stayed in Europe two weeks longer than I planned, I'm almost broke, and I am torn by the pull of my mother expecting me home. I'm all she's got since dad died last year, and my familial sense of duty is in major conflict with the Slavic princess who set my heart on fire. As my eyes scan the passing faces on the Mala Strana, hunger begins to grind in my stomach, but I'm afraid to leave the lobby.

Last night I was asked to enlist in the drug trade across the way by an odd-smelling gypsy with a threatening scar across his left cheek. The notion of some fast cash that could extend my stay was tempting, but the gypsy's dark eyes scared me more than my empty pockets. When I turned him down, his face twisted into that now familiar look of quizzical disdain Europeans often hold for Americans.

The tart aroma of ammonia in the cleaning lady's bucket snaps me out of my reverie. I am definitely not at the Palace hotel. I am one notch above a hostel, I'm down to my last thousand *koruna*, and let's face it, Katrina's never coming. What a bummer.

I'm lonely and hungry. My heart is breaking and my poor mother is probably worried sick about me. I'm screwed. Okay, that's it. I am going to buy a bottle of cheap wine and my last ever herring sandwich, catch the next train to Paris and fly home.

When I grab my bag and say goodbye, Marek jumps off his stool, "No, no! Stay! We have the good times, my friend. Prague is best party in Europe. Stay one week more. I give you discount."

Jim Bob

August 4th was the worst day of Jim Bob
Mecklenberg's life. He woke up all sticky with sweat and
anxiety, the result of a series or worrisome thoughts and
sadnesses in the night, combined with a record heat wave in
a region of South Carolina already known for stifling
summer months. He opened one eye to a slit and allowed
the first stab of early morning light to pierce his brain. The

buzzing of unseen insects had already begun, and a layer of dust created by the disturbance of the dawn freight train was visible in the air, illuminated by shafts of lights broken into beams by the saplings to the east of his window. This anxious state of mind had been growing in Jim Bob's heart for a couple of years now developing a powerful, irresistible urge to leave home. But now, with the death of his mentor and friend, he was more disposed than ever to make his escape.

A few years back, The Colonel, as he was known around those parts, had returned after a fifteen-year absence to enjoy his final days in the town of his birth. The notion in the old man's mind had been to pass on to the young folks in town some of the learning he'd accumulated through an lifetime of world travel and a series of diverse occupations ranging from able seaman to cartographer to big game safari guide. If Jim Bob had his druthers (and didn't have to look after the mountain of chores that momma laid out for him), he would have spent every minute of every day and night enjoying tales of adventure and romance from around the world. Everyone in Jacob's Village had heard the legendary tales of the Colonel's exploits since they were knee-high to a grasshopper, so when he returned home to live out his final years, people came from far and wide to catch a glimpse of the legendary town father, and if they were lucky, listen in on a tale or two. Jim Bob had the good fortune of having his mid-teen years coincide with the Colonel's return.

The town's living legend had received several generous and impressive offers to luxuriate in comfort in the plantation houses of some of the region's richest families, but with no surviving kinfolk in town since his lazy, greedy relatives had sold off the historical family home and moved north ('where they belonged' he was heard to say), he preferred to reside far from power and wealth in a rented room on the ground floor of Mrs. Henderson's, where folks could come to relax under the ceiling fans, listen to stories and enjoy two or three fingers of Jim Beam and a cheroot on a summer evening. Mrs. Henderson would never permit young Jim Bob to sample those adult pleasures, and even thought the Colonel took an instant liking to the boy, he was never allowed anything stronger than lemonade. He was disposed to accept her decision for two reasons: he had been brainwashed as a toddler to respect one's elders, and, his single stolen sip of bourbon in her kitchen one afternoon made him instantly nauseous. He was beyond happy to simply sit at The Colonel's knee and raptly absorb the endless episodes of danger, wisdom, courage, and intrigue. Jim Bob spent countless afternoons and evenings on the wraparound, screened-in porch of Mrs. Henderson's large, white, boarding house with the hundred-year-old beech tree out front drinking in chapter after chapter of an epic life well told, sitting quietly among the faithful who regularly gathered. Jim Bob could not imagine that any one man could have done all those many things, been so many places, and met so many people in one lifetime. For almost four years The Colonel declined invitations to social events, hunting excursions and motor trips, preferring to sit in his rocking chair on the porch and talk all evening to whomever made the effort to visit.

The Colonel finally breathed his last breath in his sleep after a particularly raucous yet educational evening on the porch. Mrs. Henderson called Jim Bob's momma first thing in the morning and asked her to relay the news, knowing the boy would want to be the first one to know. Aware that her boy could be a right fearful monster if he was awakened before his time, Mrs. Mecklenberg waited for Jim Bob to finish his full nine hours of sleep before gently tapping on her son's door. With mixed, very personal feelings of her own about the passing of The Colonel, she poked her head in and softly delivered the news. As she expected, Jim Bob reacted like he'd been run over by a semi rig, curling back over on his bed and facing the wall. He held in his tears until she closed the door again and he didn't leave his small bedroom for two days, grieving over the enormous chasm in his meager life now that his idol was gone. On the third day, his momma informed him through the door about the wake. He grunted from his fetal position and didn't move a muscle, but the minute he heard her feet leave his door he was up digging in his closet for that proper jacket he never wore. He could hear his momma all over the house making a big noise about getting ready, talking to herself and slamming doors and drawers like she had a beehive in her bonnet. He waited for his mother to quiet down and go into her own room. Then he quick took a shower, dressed, and exited out the back door into the torture that was high noon in summer below the Mason-Dixon line.

As if saying goodbye to his mentor wasn't the single most difficult ordeal of Jim Bob's young life, the day of Colonel Tolliver's wake was a full fifteen degrees above the already sweltering average that summer. Ochre-tinted dust hung in the air like cigar smoke at a card game. The birds were silent and butterflies stayed home. It felt like the entire county was holding its breath. The hand-me-down sports jacket that Jim Bob wore about once a year was already soaked from the inside. His equally unused lace-up shoes stabbed at his feet in several places as he trudged, taking the long way across town in order to avoid the main street where people were likely to be. He could have ridden with Momma, but something was bugging her that morning which had nothing to do with him, so he avoided her company.

Despite her nagging being at its worst lately, he was determined to break his own news to her today. He'd turned eighteen, and he had a plan. He was far from an adventurer like his mentor, but those evenings at The Colonel's knee had inspired the notion in him that he might just make something of himself if he could get away from Jacob's Village. His plan was to matriculate at the junior college up in Slocum and hopefully one day transfer to UT or Chapel Hill. Jim Bob knew that telling Momma he was going to college was worse than confessing he was a communist or a queer, and furthermore, he knew from a lifetime of lying to

her that she was unlikely to believe him anyway, so he had
already decided to make up a story more palatable for her
ears. Momma had a twisted, unalterable view of life based
on guilt and duty, and she would never, ever comprehend
his deep longing to break out of this place.

He had never lived anywhere but the house he was
born in. Hell, he'd never even been anywhere outside of
Jacob's Village. He'd always wanted to travel north to visit
his kinfolk up in Slocum, but Jim Bob's momma wouldn't
allow it, referring to their cousin Leslie as 'a slob, and not
to be trusted.' Momma always insisted that rare family
visits occur at her own house, a four-room ramshackle
wooden square whose only luxury was indoor plumbing.
Nonetheless, it was neat and properly tidy seven days a
week thanks to his momma's constant dissatisfaction with
the state of the world. Jim Bob felt a certain guilt at the
thought of leaving his momma high and dry like his older
brother had. He reckoned correctly that his overwrought
mother would certainly weep herself to sleep for God
knows how many nights (or weeks), but there had come a
time, a crossroads, an awakening, when the importance of
his momma's feelings took a back seat to his need to make
a life for himself.

Mrs. Mecklenberg wasn't even sure her son would show up at the wake, given his moping silence since the old man died. She was only attending herself out of social propriety, but her boy would have none of that. The fact that he never gave two hoots about what other people in town thought of him gave her fits. God knows she'd done everything humanly possible to prepare him for the realities of adulthood, but her efforts at discipline had been for naught. His head was permanently ensconced in the clouds. It bewildered her that he could spend so much time sitting on Mrs. Henderson's porch listening to that sly old codger rattle on about his alleged exploits. Jim Bob had once tried to explain to her the lure of The Colonel's company, but she wouldn't hear it, loudly and vehemently insisting there was nothing her son could learn from an old man who never raised a family and kept changing jobs all the time.

Now that his idol had passed away, Mrs. M's heart told her that her boy would be leaving home soon. Being a small town denizen with a certain amount of God-given wisdom, she understood these things about life and growing up, even though this knowledge brought her close to tears now and then. What the hell, he'd turned eighteen and legally, he could do as he pleased. Who knows what he's got up his sleeve. It didn't matter, really. The only person who could reveal the truth of his ancestry was gone now and it was time to move on. I gave him my best, she thought.

She was putting the finished touches on her makeup and pinning a small, round hat to her thick black hair. She hated makeup and hats, and looking at the mirror always caused her discomfort, even though her dark blue, dotted dress, a hand-me-down from her mother, accomplished the task of hiding the signs of her aging figure. She made one last, frustrated stab with the hatpin and gave up. She knocked once on Jim Bob's door and heard nothing. She went outside and wiped the dust off the driver's seat of her Ford 150 with the rag hung on the door handle for just that purpose, remembering that that had been Jim Bob's idea. I guess keeping after him wasn't a total waste of time, she chuckled to herself. It was a tossup whether she should leave the truck's windows open to let out the heat or closed the keep out the dust. It was a short run, so she kept them closed so she wouldn't have to shake her skirt clean in front of everyone when she arrived.

Practically every resident showed up to pay their respects at the ladies' auxiliary building between the church and Rev. Staunton's manse on Elm Street, the only structure in the county large enough to contain the anticipated throng of mourners. The Colonel had not been a church-going man, but the Baptist elders considered social ambition a form of piousness, and they volunteered to host the ceremony to hop on the bandwagon of respect garnered by the deceased.

Jim Bob continued on his slow trek across town to join the grieving throng, stopping only once to give directions to a sedan crammed with three generations of a family of strangers, all dressed in their Sunday finery. The news had spread quickly and wide, inspiring scores of folks to make the journey from as far as Manassas and Knoxville and Augusta to pay their respects to The Colonel. This Dixie-wide pilgrimage was testimony to the reputation of a man who had never held public office, never served in the armed forces (despite his moniker), and hadn't been seen inside a church since his first Holy Communion. Jim Bob made sure his route did not pass the Henderson place. Seeing that empty rocking chair would be too much for the boy to stomach. He was already dreading the wickedest blow to his splintered feelings when he would have to succumb to tradition and lay eyes on the great man lying inert in a box.

When you're young, the world is what it is. It ain't supposed to change. The people in the world are the people in the world. That fact that one of them could just stop being there caused Jim Bob untold consternation. He refused to accept that a person could one day be giving the soundest advice in the clearest voice with the kindest eyes in creation, then suddenly become a bundle of skin and bones. It made his mind feel all muddy, like shallow pond water mucked up by wading through it.

Jim Bob walked across town as slowly as he could while still managing to make forward progress. He had never known anyone who died; anyone close, that is. He had experienced loss at the age of six, when his father decided he'd rather play the banjo in New Orleans than put up with his wife and 'two brats and a bastard.' Jim Bob never understood what his papa meant by that remark, but he surely knew about the willful variety of abandonment, having spent most of his youth with only his half-cocked older brothers as a masculine presence in the house. But abandonment by death was another bucket of barley altogether. He couldn't seem to stop his mind from ruminating about it, even for a few minutes. He was smart enough to understand that the end of life was a comprehensible fact in terms of scientific logic and biology and so forth, but there remained a part of his nature that had difficulty arranging this information into any kind of order that didn't make him sad as hell.

He'd had a difficult time sleeping since the day of The Colonel's demise, and he hadn't spoken to anyone except his Momma (not counting his phone call to cousin Leslie), because he knew the minute he uttered one query or feeling he would be bombarded with the same old God and Heaven and Pearly Gates baloney he'd been letting float out his other ear since about age nine, when it struck him like a left jab to the forehead that all that bible mythology was no more than a grand tale people loved to tell one another so they'd have something to talk about besides their own disappointments – words spoken in the preservation of their sanity, if you will – and, of course, for the purpose of social acceptance, which meant nothing to Jim Bob in spite of the fact that every soul in Jacob's Village believed otherwise. The Colonel eschewed the word 'believe.' He preferred to say, "Reflecting on the accumulated evidence from my own personal experience, it occurs to me that [such and such] is probably true [or false]." He never subscribed to any religious folderol and yet he was probably the most spiritually advanced man in the whole piedmont. He was fair to everyone and lived without rancor or pretense. He shared his time and wisdom with people of all races, ages, religious persuasions and political points of view. The Colonel's greatest gift to Jim Bob was a strong foundation of universal wisdom and humanity.

Jim Bob continued to make his way across town in a daze, kicking pine needles aside and tasting the grit of clay dust between his molars. He almost forgot about the Tuckers' half-crazy Rottweiler, that insane killing machine that leapt up against their fence, barking and foaming all over himself. That jarred Jim Bob out of his reverie and back to the present, not that he wanted to be. If he never made it to the wake at all that would be okay with him. He did not want to see the physical evidence that The Colonel was gone forever, and he doubly didn't want to face Momma. This was the day they'd both been dreading, each for their own reasons. Momma refused to contemplate the idea her boy was fixing to leave; deluding herself into hoping that his mood of recent weeks was due to the old man's imminent deceasement (she liked to make up words).

Jim Bob felt like crying but his eyes remained dry. He wanted to cry out of fear of the future, of the loss of his only friend, and of leaving his Momma in an empty house. But no one in his family ever cried. His Momma had told him many times that crying was a sign of weakness, that one oughtn't make a fuss and draw attention to oneself. It was almost as if there was a specific gene in her DNA that prevented her from admitting to any kind of pain. He had sneaked a peek at her crying once, back when he was six, right after his father ran off. She didn't know anybody was watching when she allowed this very last show of emotion, smack in the middle of which she stopped her bawling, sat up straight, wiped her eyes, and went back to fixing dinner for her boys.

When her two oldest took off for the Marine Corps and the Galveston shrimp boats, respectively, both in the same week, Momma lifted up her chin and smiled, wished them luck and even gave them sack lunches for the first leg of their journeys. She blew her nose a lot that week and drank cup after cup of hot tea with lemon, but she never said anything to anybody except that she was proud her sons had "ventured forth," as she put it, "to test their capabilities in the world of strangers." When Jim Bob asked her if she missed them, all she said was, "Oh, they'll be fine. I taught 'em well. They know how to fend for themselves. They'll be fine."

Jim Bob's circuitous route to the wake took him past the remaining chimney of the Ralston place, where the only girl he had ever loved used to live. The charred remains were overgrown with brambles, and Jim Bob knew that one day even the chimney would be smothered by vines and shadowed by trees growing straight up through the old floor of the house. Eventually all traces of the Ralstons would be covered over, like a memory receding into the back of one's mind with the accumulation of time and further experiences. When their house burned down, Beth's ultra-religious father claimed it was a sign from God and immediately moved the entire family to Chicago, of all places. Most folks in town thought that decision was a bit radical, but it was generally accepted that religious fanatics had at least one screw loose. Beth wrote to him for a few months, but her letters ebbed to a trickle and eventually stopped. It tore at him not to pursue her, but being only thirteen years old at the time rendered that quest pretty much out of the question. This was a very lucky and serendipitous time in Jim Bob's young life, since the homecoming of Colonel Tolliver happily interrupted his grieving over Beth and the end of his impossible dream of true love. The powerful presence of the man who would forever alter his way of thinking helped Jim Bob move past his broken heart and focus his passion on his mind and his future.

Seeing that solitary chimney among the ruins of the Ralston house reminded him of the time he and Beth were walking the long way home on a spring afternoon after school and they came upon a bone half buried in some loose, damp earth in the part of the woods where the sun hardly ever shone. They couldn't decide whether the relic was human or from some large animal. There were stories about bears and cougars in the region, but no one had actually seen one. They vowed to each other they wouldn't tell anyone they'd found it. It was their first, last, and only secret. He wondered at the time if that meant they were in love. She seemed to take their sworn oath pretty seriously, but he couldn't be sure and was afraid to ask. They entertained conjecture about the history of that bone, with neither of them willing to insist it was human, even though they both knew it was. He had wondered to himself about the soul of the being that had once occupied the marrow of that bone. He had silently asked himself if the sum total of an entire human life ended up being a bone that two kids come upon in the woods one day? It hadn't occurred to him at the time how odd it was to find a human bone, all by itself, in the middle of the woods. It was just one more queer event associated with the Ralston family. He suspected that Beth had broken her vow and told her father about finding the bone, and that motivated Mr. Ralston's sudden decision to head north. There are several large gaps in the story of the Ralston family. Many of the local pundits wondered if their house fire was truly an accident. Jim Bob was always thinking about things like that.

As he continued his reluctant march to the Colonel's penultimate resting place, the mystery of the Ralston family gave way in his mind to the dread he felt in anticipation of talking to Momma. He was so lost in thought he almost walked into a spider web, but the sun glinted off it at the last second and he reeled away, avoiding one more abuse of the most physically uncomfortable day of his young life. He stopped for a minute to examine the insects that lay stuck, dead in the geometric web and thought about the food chain

– the bugs and the birds and the worms and the vermin and he wondered if any of them had souls. He wondered how they knew how to build nests and hide nuts and weave those amazing webs. He recalled how Buster, the now-departed family spaniel, seemed almost human when he tilted his head and looked up at Jim Bob when he wanted to be petted. He thought about all the times that dog had approached him when he was feeling down and wondered if Buster knew his master needed some company? Did domestic animals exist on a higher spiritual plane than wild ones? It occurred to him that pets spend less time worrying about survival than wild animals do, so perhaps they develop some kind of intelligence in the relative security of a human home. Although Jim Bob could not stop the constant speculation about such things, he certainly would never bring them up in conversation. He figured out early on that most things were just not worth mentioning. People start asking too many questions and it never seems to end. He understood it was human nature to want to know stuff, but his considered opinion was that most folks he knew asked questions to advance their own status in the shallow world of gossip and wasted time. Jim Bob was interested in galactic things; grand, cosmic things. He wanted to know about the stars and why people do what they do. He wanted to ride in an airplane and swim in the ocean. He wanted to meet people from other countries. With the exception of the small, reverent coterie of admirers gathered on Mrs. Henderson's porch when The Colonel was holding forth, talking to adults bored Jim Bob. Most grownups only wanted to hear things that reinforced what they already thought. They didn't really want to know about the things that raised questions in Jim Bob's mind; they weren't interested in *learning*.

All this thinking almost made him turn around and go home. He really didn't want to spend even one half-second sitting around with a bunch of people trying to look like they cared, trying to look good for one another, trying to do what was expected of them without giving one single thought to the essence of the ritual and the depth of meaning to this great man's life. Now *there* was something to be sad about – folks gathering under the auspices of the funeral to enhance their own status. Jim Bob, on the other hand, was showing up because he truly loved The Colonel and this would be his final opportunity to say farewell and thank you, Sir.

Rather than enter the ladies' auxiliary straight away, Jim Bob stood outside against the clapboard wall in a small patch of shade near one of the open windows. He listened to that formal, soft, chitchatty hum typical of these occasions; every variety of murmured nicety, said in good faith but routinely, harmonizing with the raspy, impaired breathing of the elderly.

He involuntarily leaned toward the window, thinking he heard his momma's voice. It was then that he noticed a tear in the corner of the screen, out of which crawled a small yellow spider with black stripes on her legs. He watched as she side-stepped away from the muted conversations and the human smells that identified this crowded room as no place to construct a web. She carefully made her way down the outside wall, one white clapboard at a time, deftly detouring around jutting nailheads and thick flakes of old paint, finally disappearing into a small opening that led under the house where it was dark and damp and twenty degrees cooler.

Jim Bob entered the former Staunton mansion by its rear entrance, careful not to let the screen door slam behind him. He cut through the kitchen where several Baptist volunteers were organizing covered dishes, icing tea and lemonade, and discussing how long the desserts would hold up in this heat. A couple of the chubby ladies, wiping their hands of their auxiliary aprons, smiled politely and greeted Jim Bob with an appropriately earnest demeanor, acknowledging his well-known relationship with the dearly departed. Jim Bob appreciated the sincerity of their kindness and managed to pause and squeeze a perfunctory smile in the corner of his mouth. He nodded back, blinked, glanced at the floor, then continued on across the kitchen. He turned and opened the door to the main room, with its worn, shiny, oak board floor, and familiar, sparse décor; a framed drawing of Jefferson Davis on one wall and a print of a painting of Jesus opposite. The air in the great room was hot but not dusty, and there was a large floor fan in the far corner trying to jostle the heat around. The window screens were doing a middling job, as he'd seen for himself, limiting the indoor insect population to half a dozen house flies.

Having entered from the kitchen, he suddenly found himself standing directly next to the coffin. He simply turned left and there was The Colonel, lying on the pleated satin lining in his finest pinstriped, seersucker suit, his hands folded across his belt. His right ring finger was adorned with the beautiful yet masculine Carnelian ring Jim Bob had always admired. A rush of guilt flushed his face when he remembered wishing The Colonel had given him that ring before he passed away. What a waste that such a perfect, manly piece of jewelry should be interred forever. The undertaker probably believed that it would suit The Colonel in the afterlife. Jim Bob loathed that sort of non-thinking rubbish. He breathed deeply as he gazed into the open casket. A series of tingles raised the hair on his arms. The Colonel's head rested on a tiny, cushioned platform, his graying, ginger hair combed neatly back and waxed into place. His peaceful face had been made to look oddly paralyzed by the undertaker's cosmetics. Jim Bob's brain swirled with the existential questions that had been haunting him for days without settling on a single one. As his eyes blurred out of focus, his reverie was interrupted by a gentle, polite nudge on his elbow. He turned to see a line of people waiting to pay their respects. He ceded his spot before the casket, turned away and walked slowly to the opposite side of the room, where he accepted his temporary fate, a seat on a folding chair against the wall next to his mother. A stranger would never have known they were related, what with her straight, jet-black hair and her boy with his freckles and rust-colored curls. Jim Bob decided to be silent and wait for an opportunity.

"It took you long enough to get here."

Jim Bob's face went blank, a practiced reflex to Momma's tone. He stared at the mole on her chin.

"Sit up straight." Jim Bob adjusted his posture about a quarter of an inch, followed by a brief silence of no particular significance.

"When's the food comin' out? I'm flat out starved."

"In due time, young man, in due time." Momma always gave the same answer to any question with the word "when" in it. "Not that you'd appreciate a homemade dish, mister red licorice and Dr. Pepper three meals a day. How's anyone to know you was raised proper?"

"I swear I'd eat a tractor tire right about now."

Mrs. M gave him a look that acknowledged her boy was one of a kind and unlikely to change. She looked him over, knowing full well he'd got his gumption up and was fixing to fly the coop. She was slightly worried he might turn into a rootless, no-account like his wandering father, but mainly she knew in her heart that she was going miss that boy something fierce. She sat silently, waiting for him to tell her his mind.

The stifling heat and close quarters made him extremely fidgety. Jim Bob squirmed in his seat a few times. He was aware of the hum of the fan in the corner and the creaking of a loose floorboard here and there. He saw Mrs. Humbolt across the room with her matching outfit and large hat, working the crowd for donations for her so-called charity. And there was old Jefferson Wilkins, once the playboy of Piedmont County back in the fifties, working his worn-out charm on the ladies from the assisted living center who'd been bussed over from Catersville for the occasion. Jim Bob was contemplating how long it must've taken to unload that small bus full of walkers and wheelchairs when his momma finally spoke up. "You know what I'm gonna miss most about not havin' The Colonel around?"

Without turning to look at her, Jim Bob said, "What's that, Momma?"

"Ain't gonna be nobody hereabouts for you to look up to no more, that's what."

Jim Bob squeezed that fact around in his overcrowded brain, causing a memory to plop out of his subconscious and onto his tongue. "He taught me how to whittle, y'know."

"That's just lovely, son. Did he mention anything 'bout make a livin' with that jackknife?"

Jim Bob contemplated his Momma's obsession with finding fault.

"If you'd just do somethin' with your lazy self, git a job, somethin."

This was it. The perfect time to tell her what was on his mind. He cleared his throat and began his reply, "As a matter of fact..."

Just then Judge McElroy stopped before them and bowed his gaunt, six-foot-six frame down to Mrs. Mecklenberg, the wispy remains of a full head of hair falling in front of his eyes like he planned it that way, whereupon she extended her hand for a dramatic kiss, a ritual she knew he favored.

"Good aft'noon, ma'am," he drawled. "Mighty pleased to see you, although I do regret the circumstances couldn't be more convivial."

She smiled, knowing what he wanted (he was a man, after all, never mind being on the far side of 70). He'd been sniffin' around regular since Mr. M. had skipped, never missing a Sunday bake sale at First Baptist. Momma created a smile, dismissing the judge with a tiny hint of 'welcome back' in her grin, ever so slightly allowing him to infer some vague future opportunity. Hizzoner smiled back, stood up straight, brushed strands of white hair away from his eyes, nodded perfunctorily to Jim Bob, and moved on down the row of ladies in folding chairs, kissing the mostly gloved hands and complimenting the elaborate hats of the widows and maiden aunts. Jim Bob waited a polite minute after the Judge left before he spoke again to his Momma.

"I'm goin' on up to Slocum t'morrow."

Momma smirked, "Is it possum season already?"

"Cousin Leslie called yesterd'y, says there might be some work up 'ere."

"That no 'count slouch? He ain't never done nothin' for nobody didn't have sumpin' in it for hisself."

"Says there's a new shoppin' mall goin' up just off the Interstate. Might be some security positions available."

"'Security positions?' She snickered. "I daresay they ain't nuthin' worth guardin' within a hunnert miles of that two-bit hog farm."

"Maybe so, but if it's a job, I'ma take it."

She slowly turned in her chair to face her son.

"Look at it this way, Momma; I'll be outa your hair and makin' my own money. Won't be a burden to you no more."

"We'll see." She looked close at Jim Bob's eyes and saw he meant what he said. "I don't trust yer cousin Leslie, is all. When it comes to yer father's side of the family, you bes' be wary, you hear?' Jim Bob was trapped in the middle again. "Look at me, son. You hear what I'm sayin'?"

"Yes, Momma, I hear."

Well, that wasn't so hard, he thought. What was I worrying about all morning? Maybe Momma's right; maybe I think too much. No matter. Jim Bob allowed half a minute to elapse so his final escape wouldn't necessarily appear to be motivated by her constant aggravation. He couldn't wait to hit the road but he didn't want to hurt her feelings. "Will you excuse me, please? I gotta go visit the convenience."

"Wash your hands after."

As he stood up and adjusted his ill-fitting sports jacket, he leaned over close to his mother's ear and spoke so only she could hear. "Keep an eye on the Colonel for me, will ya, Momma?"

"You bite your tongue, boy," she whispered, covering a grin with her gloved hand. Sometimes that child *was* funny. Mrs. Mecklenberg watched her youngest lope toward the rear of the large room. She noticed he turned his eyes away from the casket as he passed it. She felt a tear roll down her cheek. Nobody took any notice, it being a funeral and all.

My Sister

My sister and I took our little boat out on the lake every day of every summer of our childhood. I did the rowing while she sat in the stern. Rowboats are funny like that. Only one person can row. As her older brother, this duty fell to me, but make no mistake, I enjoyed it. I proudly assumed the role of man of the family when our father had died of leukemia when I was eight years old. Sarah was just six. My mother's smile was sad and sympathetic as she watched me take my new responsibility very seriously. I did not realize at the time that us kids were a distraction from the grief I couldn't understand.

Our family's rowboat was wooden and painted red – that shade of faded red you used to see on barns and tee shirts back then. It's got a little maroon in it and some brown, but mostly it's red. You don't hardly see that color nowadays. Back in the 1960s things were painted once when they were new and never again. Paint faded and chipped off after a while and that was okay. To this day whenever I see that color on a faded tee shirt or an old boat, my mind floats back to those lazy, bright, innocent times that will always be my favorite memories. The oars had never been painted so they turned that aged grey that wood becomes when it's constantly exposed to the elements over the years. The oarlocks were oxidized stainless steel and the sockets were worn wide from use, causing them to make a clop, clonk sound as I rowed. Whenever I recall those summers in upstate New York, I can still hear the rhythm of those oarlocks echoing across the empty lake in the morning, the sound of adventure ahead.

Sarah let her imagination run wild in the boat: she'd pretend to be a princess, adjusting her tiara and arranging the folds of her regal robe, her imaginary silk skirts spread out and covering her half of our royal craft. She once made me a knight, tapping me on each shoulder with a wet tree branch. When I told her the story of Cleopatra I'd learned in school, she pretended she was seated on a gilded barge as it floated down the Nile, its banks lined with worshipful subjects hoping for a glimpse of their queen. Her Royal Highness's favorite sport, and mine too, was exploring the natural wonders along our lake's miles of shaded, mossy banks. We never tired of checking out the beetles, the darting schools of fish, and the perpetually green, damp, otherworldly growths under the natural awnings created by the huge trees along the shore. Sometimes I stopped rowing and we just drifted around in the middle of the lake, lying back with our eyes closed, our fingers tracing the surface of the water, the sun's warmth soothing our faces. The silence was pure. Barely noticeable breezes caressed our skin as we listened to musical conversations between the orioles and warblers.

Sarah and I treasured our status of being united together and apart from everyone else. It made us feel special and we knew it. But Sarah went a step further. Before she was ten years old, my sister had instinctively developed the ability to experience deep joy. I watched in awe as she'd get an idea and forget all about pretending. She would recline in the back of the boat, face up, and let the sun heat up her imagination. I could only guess at her thoughts. We did not know it at the time, but Sarah had organically learned how to meditate. She would lie there in silence, her face glowing with the contentment of a Buddhist. She worshipped the sun. She called it the source of all nature, as she explained to me one summer when she had suddenly acquired the ability to speak like an intellectual, "without which there would be no lake, no trees, no Nile, and no gold to be fashioned into my royal crown."

Dad had taught me how to fish when I was five and Sarah was still a toddler. After five years of watching me, she suddenly insisted she wanted to learn herself, so I rowed us to dad's special corner of the lake. As the man of the house, I recounted to my eight-year-old sister my father's informative lecture about this section of the lake, where the water was the deepest and the fish were rumored to grow uncommonly large.

Once we reached that special fishing spot, I continued my fishing lesson. In the middle of my lecture on the finer points of bait, a wriggling worm startled Sarah and she stumbled backwards, over the gunwale and into the water. She hadn't learned to swim yet and she panicked. I jumped in and used my YMCA training to drag her to the bank, which was closer, because her fall and my dive had propelled our boat away from the shore quite a way out into the lake. After I planted her on dry land and assured her she would survive, I swam out to the boat, found the oar that had fallen in the water, and rowed back to Sarah. She was more scared than hurt, but that embarrassing moment fueled her determination to conquer worms and water and everything else. Within a week she had taught herself to swim like a dolphin, and to this day Sarah's the only girl I've ever known who could spear a baitworm onto a fish hook without qualms. Her plethora of childhood achievements included such diverse feats as the family distance record for skipping stones across the water and the invention of peanut butter and licorice sandwiches.

Anchored about fifty yards out from our house's dock was an ancient, wooden floating platform that had been built and moored long before our family began spending summers at the lake. Its ladder had two rungs missing, and a couple of planks on the top had disappeared as well, but Sarah and I didn't know any better. For all we knew, all lake platforms had blank spaces and broken rungs. I was really glad Sarah learned to swim, because when it got really hot, we could swim out to the float and play together for hours; jumping, diving, and playing tag or king of the hill. Sometimes we raced back to shore. Even though she was younger and a girl, she beat me every time, except when I insisted we swim backstroke and she got water up her nose. One summer I found a garden snake in the woods and couldn't resist hiding it in her bed. Sarah knew darn well they were harmless, but she pretended to be all scared and mad at me just so she could get mother to give her extra Graham crackers. Then she made up a rule that if I publicly apologized to her she would share the Grahams with me. She was always doing stuff like that. I may have been the man of the house, but she was in charge of our life together. On the rare rainy days when we couldn't enjoy the lake, we invented games, told each other scary stories, and giggled until we could hardly breathe. Sometimes we just sat in the boat in the middle of the lake, turned our faces skyward and let the rain soak us. Those were the days.

Ever since dad went to heaven (so we were told), leaving us semi-orphans, Mother's mantra had become, "I

don't know what I'd do without you kids." We did our best
to make mother proud and show her how much we
appreciated her taking care of us. Even though we were
children and couldn't grasp the concept of death, our young
hearts sensed how difficult it was for mom after dad died.
When I think back on that time, his loss must have
devastated her, especially since those were the days when
couples made lifetime commitments. Her life had been
altered forever and we had become the sole source of what
little happiness she felt. Sarah and I made our beds and did
our chores every morning, making mom smile with
gratitude and earning our right to play and explore all day
long. Mother insisted we come back to the cabin for lunch
no matter what we were doing or how far away we were.
She made us her famous luncheon meat sandwiches with
American cheese and Gulden's mustard every day. She also
let us scarf down all the walnuts and seedless grapes we
could stomach. To this day, the tastes of Waldorf salads
evoke in me that same pang of nostalgia as the memory of
faded red rowboats. She served our splendid lunches on
plastic plates that we washed ourselves and put away before
we waved goodbye to mom and marched back down to the
dock. We knew by heart every inlet, every rock, every

overhanging branch, and every piece of property on that lake. Most of our neighbors waved and smiled when we rowed past their docks, but a few of the year-round folks didn't really cotton to us summer people and pretended not to see us. When we cruised past them they would roll their eyes and get busy refilling their lemonades or hike up the intensity of their badminton games.

I'll never forget the hot summer evening my little sister stood towering over me. I had fainted. Mom's attempt at a special treat – spinach salad with bay shrimp – turned out to be a disaster. The first thing my eyes saw when I came to was Sarah's face, holding simultaneous looks of empathy and fear, neither of which was going to save her big brother from his first allergy attack. I had eaten bushels of shrimp every summer without so much as a hiccup. Suddenly, I had been turned into a swollen, itchy, dizzy mess from a few forkfuls of shellfish. The anti-inflammatories helped, but Sarah holding my hand did more for my recovery than any medicine ever could. I took my time getting well to prolong the special attention from my two ladies. They both knew I was malingering, but they never let on. Sarah sat indoors on the chair in our bedroom and read me stories, while mom continually replenished the walnuts and grapes and Graham crackers.

We both hated going back to the suburbs in September. One Labor Day weekend Sarah and I marched into the kitchen together, holding hands, a bold, miniature phalanx, and petitioned mother to let us stay at the lake all year long.

"But my darlings, the lake is frozen over all winter and the cabin and the roadways are covered with snow taller than both of you."

We frowned and insisted, "Mo-om."

"And," she added, "the only source of heat in this cabin is the wood-burning stove."

That reminder ended our weak plea. Our eyes met and we both reached the same, sensible conclusion simultaneously. We weren't afraid of twelve feet of snow but we hadn't considered having to chop a winter's worth of wood. Besides, who would make the sandwiches? We sheepishly went back to packing up the car, accepting our fate of yet another suburban winter.

One year, everything changed. Those famously irrational years of puberty and adolescence arrived and

Sarah's personality began to flourish. I wasn't much affected by the change, what with all my responsibilities around the house, but Sarah took on a whole new aspect. She spent hours at the library. She wore girly clothes. She took art classes after school. She never seemed to be home. When she did manage to join mom and me for dinner, we had great conversations, fanning the embers of hope that she might still be the best friend I had grown up with. But when dinner was over, she went back to being the new Sarah with the changing body and capricious temperament. When I dared mention my feelings, she swore she still loved me like a brother, but she was developing strong interests elsewhere. She no longer went to Ranger games at The Garden with me. I took my best shot and invited her to see the van Gogh exhibit at the Met, but she had already been there with one of her pot-smoking, bearded friends from Greenwich Village. She shared Polaroids of them with me that mom never saw. When she was home, she spent all her time upstairs painting and drawing and talking on the phone.

The following June was the worst day of my life (at the time). Sarah announced on the last day of school that she didn't want to go to our cabin on the lake for the summer. I couldn't imagine going to the lake alone. I looked at mom for support, but she just shrugged the way I imagine all mom's do when their children grow up. That corner of my mind where I stuffed my disappointments was becoming quite crowded. I couldn't imagine going to the lake without Sarah, so we stayed in the same boring suburbs after school let out. I spent the summer helping mom do maintenance work on our house while she made a half-hearted stab at a career working part time at a local real estate office. When Sarah wasn't in her room talking on the phone, she was continually taking the train into the city, often staying overnight, going to art shows and parties with her many boyfriends. She was only fifteen and I feared for her safety, but mother convinced me that Sarah had a mind of her own and was more capable at taking care of herself than most adults. There was one upside to Sarah's frequent absences; my mother and I cooked dinner together most nights and I got to know her in a different way. I was becoming an adult and mom felt safe sharing her feelings with me. She never quite revealed her deepest grief about our dad or her life as a widow, but she allow me a glimpse of the evolution of her life: her happy times, her expectations and disappointments. She seemed relieved to have someone to talk to and I saw my mother for the first time as a fellow human being.

When the time came, I wasn't motivated to apply to colleges. Sarah overheard me talking to mother about it and pulled me upstairs and into her room. She closed the door, sat me down, and insisted that I do something for myself for a change. She reminded me that she'd be leaving home in a year anyway, on account of having skipped ninth grade. I couldn't argue with her. She always knew better than I did what was best for me. I wanted to go to Columbia or NYU, but she insisted I pick a school far away. We compromised on the University of Chicago.

It turned out to be a great school in a great city, but neither the curriculum nor the heartland ever captured my interest. I couldn't concentrate. I stayed sane by channeling my energy into rowing. The university had just initiated a rowing team, so the muscles and technique I developed on the lake earned me a spot on the double scull crew. I never declared a major, but I did pledge a fraternity. I liked most of the guys and the sense of belonging, but every weekend they threw rollicking keg parties that transformed these future Nobel laureates and captains of industry into screaming, gyrating, barfing idiots. Don't get me wrong, I like a good party, but in the end I'm a rowboat kind of guy. I often locked myself in my room, put on headphones and wrote letters to Sarah. After a year and a half of C+/B- boredom, I finally gave up and returned to Putnam County.

Dropping out of college was probably not the smartest life decision, but my coming home turned out to be just what mother needed. Sarah had gone off to study painting in the south of France, and mother realized she didn't have the energy to maintain the perfect hairdo and forced eagerness required for success in the real estate game. She fell back into a fidgety, housebound life of mild apprehension. She lost weight and her face turned ashen. My unexpected return jumpstarted her out of her second floor room where she had been staring at her sewing machine for months without touching it. Her nurturing instincts were revived and she began to clean up and make meals. In a week the color had returned to her face. Within a month she was designing and stitching dresses at her old Singer. My clearest memory of that time will always be mother making macaroni and cheese every Tuesday dinner, like she had since I was three.

There is never a good time for bad news. Sarah called from Barcelona.

"Hello."

"Hi. I'm glad you answered."

"Where are you? This connection is lousy."

"I'm in Spain with Marco."

"Who's Marco?"

"Um… this Italian guy I've been seeing."

"Okay…" I let some silence pass, but Sarah wasn't forthcoming. I guessed this was one of those times when I just had to drag it out of her. "Is there something…?"

"Promise you won't say a word to mother."

"Come on, Sarah, you know darn well..."

"Promise!"

"Okay, okay. I promise. Now what…" She burst into tears.

"I'm too young… I can't… I'm too young…"

"Whoa. Wait a minute. Back up here. What's… Are you…?"

"I'm too young and I'm not strong enough and I love him but I can't be anyone's mother and… Oh God, I don't know, I just don't know anymore…"

I felt out of my depth, talking to my baby sister about this stuff. "Is this guy... Marco... is he the father?"

"It doesn't matter. It's over. It's gone. I'm not even going to tell him. I'm telling you. I took care of it."

My little sister, the princess from the rowboat, was calling me from Barcelona at age 18 to tell me that she'd had an affair and an abortion. I sat down.

"What are you going to do now?"

"Oh, God bless you, big brother. You always ask the right questions, eventually."

"Thanks, I guess. Sounds like a big decision."

"Yeah. It is. One of my paintings was accepted for a student show at an académie in Montparnasse. I really want to go there, too. I mean, the south of France is great and school's been great, and bumming around Europe with Marco and all, but I would love to be a real painter—in Paris—you know what I mean?"

Did I know what she meant? Boy, I sure did. If it had been anyone else but Sarah I would have been drooling with envy.

"Any chance you could come home? Mom would love..."

"No."

I was stunned by her quick response.

"I love you, brother, but there's nothing there for me anymore."

"Then I vote for Paris."

"Yeah, I was kind of thinking that already. Thanks, as usual."

"You're welcome, as usual."

"What about you? Are you going to leave home?" She laughed at her teasing remark, but she meant it and I knew she meant it. My little sis was pushing me to ditch my 'man of the house' act and stop deluding myself that Putnam County could offer me any kind of satisfactory life. But I wasn't ready to leave. Not just yet. During the silence I thought about those things, then the voice of the Spanish operator interrupted us.

"I'm out of change. I gotta run. Catch ya later. Ciao." Those were the last words I ever heard her speak, but she did keep to our agreement that whoever was away from home writes letters. She proudly informed me that her canvas won honorable mention at the show and she was given a scholarship to L'ecole des Beaux Artes. I knew the creative energy in Paris would be perfect for Sarah. She lived and worked in a narrow atelier not far from the famed

Bateau Lavoir, Picasso's former studio. Her letters were full of optimism and she claimed to be finding an original force in her work. She joked about her new obsession with Dalmatian figs and red wine. But as time wore on, her letters became shorter and less enthusiastic. She finally admitted that she felt physically weak, and mentally weary. The abortion and her tumultuous romance with the mercurial Marco had wiped her out. Standing before her easel had become too draining. In one of her last letters, she admitted that Marco had left her for another woman. Then she stopped writing. Several weeks passed without a word. I had to do something.

I climbed to the top of the stairs and stood in front of Sarah's apartment door, painted bright yellow in sharp contrast with the dreary grey hallway, lit only by a bare bulb on one of those twisty timers common to European buildings. I wondered aloud, "Why yellow?" No one answered. I found the building manager, explained myself with the help of a phrase book and asked to be let inside her flat. He looked me up and down and refused. Welcome to Paris. I took a room in a pension on the nearest square and hung out at a café within sight of her courtyard entrance. I began combing the neighborhood, struggling with my high school French, asking about Sarah. I inquired among people on her street; the gypsy flower seller, the *tabac* shop owner, patrons at the Lebanese market that sold her favorite figs. A few people recognized her picture but said they hadn't seen her around recently. For three days and nights I overdosed on coffee, slept fitfully, and never saw her, coming or going. I checked with the closest hospital and the local post office to no avail. Every day I pleaded with the manager/concierge – no luck. The American embassy was no help. My final confrontation was with a crooked little old lady with a grey moustache in a mourning dress and droopy stockings. I blocked her way as she arrived at Sarah's courtyard entrance. She defiantly jutted her chin with its hairy mole up into my face. *"Q'est-ce que vous voulez?"* She demanded. I had memorized the sentences I needed for my purpose, *"Je cherche mon souer. Elle s'appelle Sarah. Elle habite ici."* I pointed up over her shoulder to Sarah's window.

She looked at me as though I was making this story up to burglarize the place or sell drugs to her grandchildren. *"Vous êtes Englais?"* This question came up *all* the time but I just couldn't lie. *"Non, je suis Americain."* She snarled and spat near my feet. She shuffled quickly past me into her ground floor apartment and phoned the gendarmes. It must have been a slow crime day because the police arrived in one minute, sized up the situation and warned me, in words I couldn't translate but instantly understood, that I was very close to arrest and deportation. I kept a low profile in the neighborhood for one more fruitless night, left my number with the concierge and the owner of the café, walked three blocks to the big avenue, and hailed a taxi for de Gaulle airport.

Ten hours later, my standby flight landed at JFK. I struck a deal with a gypsy cabbie to take me through the city and up to Putnam County. It was after midnight when the taxi pulled up to our house. All the lights were on, upstairs and down. I could see mother framed by the kitchen window, sitting hunched over the table. It was warm and humid, but a chill swept over my entire body. I paid the driver and headed up the steps, bracing my heart for whatever was to come.

Mother sat still, silent, staring at nothing. I reached across the table and took a crumpled piece of paper from her trembling hands. I spread it open with my fingers and read her scribbles. *"Sarah - Internal bleeding -30 Sept – 2100- 9 PM?"*

We both sat there, unmoving, blankly staring into the worn wood of the hundred-year-old oak table between us. I noticed my nails were filthy. A siren wailed on the highway on the far side of town. My sad, addled brain calculated one fact: I had been there, probably only blocks away.

As I stood on the platform looking down the curving tracks to where they disappeared into the trees, I heard Paul Simon's line in my mind, "Everybody loves the sound of a train in the distance." My sister was coming home. Sarah hated black, but I wore it out of respect for mother and, I confess, to facilitate some sympathetic assistance from the station porter, as the hearse driver was too old to handle our burden. I handed the paperwork directly to mother without looking at it. Everyone else I've ever talked to has always wanted to know the details of the last hours of their beloved. I didn't see the point. I guess father's leukemia turned me into a bit of a fatalist. I can't remember how we arrived at the decision that there would be no ceremony, no memorial, and no invitations. Mother and I put her to rest alone, together.

In my initial grief, I had wanted to tear up Sarah's letters into tiny, unreadable pieces, but I didn't, thank God.

Those letters were to my heart what the earth was under my feet. For several weeks I did little else but read them over and over. Months passed as Mother and I sleepwalked through meals and soap operas, leaving mail in a heap on the table, letting the trash pile up, our infrequent steps echoing in the cavernous, empty house. The weather was getting colder, further reducing our ambition. We lived on pizza and Chinese takeout. Christmas and New Year's passed unnoticed. I only shoveled the driveway when we ran out of toilet paper or coffee.

Finally one Sunday I went to Mass for the first time in years, hoping to find something, anything to jar my spirit awake. I wanted comfort, some good-old-fashioned mercy and hope, but the service was in English and left me nostalgic and confused. I felt no solace or inspiration. The sunlight refracted by the stained glass windows poked painfully at my eyes. When the small congregation rose to move forward and partake of the Body of Christ, I stood with them but turned away and slipped out the door.

After six months of sleeping and ruminating in the hollow corners of our acre, the arrival of the first days of spring told me it was time to make a move. I felt an urge in my gut, but nothing gelled in my thoughts. The evolution of my mother's heart had carried her to a similar state of mind, and one evening, without planning it, we sat across from each other at our venerable dining table for the first time since *that* night.

"I wrote to your aunt Therese in Napa last week, and she's invited me to come out there." Mother adored her twin sister, and it turned out the timing was perfect because she needed help with a new winery venture.

"That'll be great. For how long?"

"How long? Oh, honey… I'm moving in with her."

You… you are? You're moving? You mean, to live?" I shook my head and smiled for the first time since forever. "Wow, that's… that's great."

She looked so pleased with herself. I was happy, too—and relieved. I had been worried about her, but she was in fine shape compared to me. She was eager to step into her future. I was still window-shopping.

Mother wanted to sell the house to leave the past behind and finance the next chapter of her life. She wanted to split the profits, but I couldn't take money she'd spent her life accumulating. She insisted, so I accepted one quarter of the sale price. We listed the house with her former real estate boss and I promised to see it through. The responsibility turned out to be just what I needed. I asked her if I could have the cabin. She smiled wistfully and said, "Absolutely. I was hoping you wanted it. I can't imagine anyone else there."

Mom moved to California and I found a small apartment on the upper west side of Manhattan. I landed a position as an intern at an art gallery. I thought it would be a good way to honor my sister's memory.

The following Memorial Day weekend, I stood on our little dock, staring across the lake at a huge tractor with its powerful chain wrapped around the trunk of a giant sycamore tree. The family that summered on the fancy estate across the water was yanking their majestic, eighty-foot tree out of the ground because, according to gossip in the village, it stood where they wanted to install a swimming pool. A swimming pool next to a lake? That elegant, broad tree with its large leaves was a natural landmark directly opposite our cabin that Sarah and I had used countless times to guide us safely home. We never met the people that lived there, but I remember once when we had rowed close to their shore and stopped our little boat by grabbing one of those huge branches that hang far out and drooped near the surface of the water. We looked through the tangle of twigs and leaves, spying on the big family having their big picnic. It certainly wasn't our idea of a picnic, what with their servants, shiny indoor furniture and what mom called, 'good china.' Everyone was dressed up, but they didn't look like they were having much fun, except for one red-faced older man who laughed at himself when he stumbled and knocked over a champagne bucket. Sarah and I had to cover our mouths to keep our laughter from giving us away.

I stood wistful on the opposite shore, watching the sad end of that magnificent, ancient tree that had provided shade for fancy picnics and a landmark for my sister and me. Not that it mattered. Our old rowboat was dried up. The cabin would soon belong to someone else. Maybe one day I'd be able to smile at those summer memories of my sister and me, but for now, tree or no tree, the lake might as well have been an image on a television screen, flat and empty.

Next Time, A Rabbit

I shoot blanks. I'll never have children. I warned all four of my wives straight away, but women only hear what they want to hear. Shortly after number four slammed the door behind her, I took early retirement with a modest pension from a multi-national accounting firm, a job I hated every day for thirty years. The very next morning after my gold watch party I woke up with pain in my back and left shoulder so severe I could barely make it out of bed. But this was more than just physical pain. It was a premonition that Saturday was the first day of the end of my life.

The variety, location, and degree of my pains expanded slowly and steadily. Numbness, tingling and cramps in my hands and feet kept me awake to all hours. When I did sleep, I was often startled awake by wheezing and abdominal cramps. My joints were immobilized to the point that it took me five minutes to maneuver my socks and shoes onto my feet. I moved everything in the house to waist-high cabinets to avoid having to reach up or bend over. The postman rudely suggested I might be a depressed hypochondriac, but I didn't need a postal worker *or* a doctor to tell me that the intense pain throughout my body was very real and signaled my inevitable demise.

I lived alone, so no one heard my intermittent cries of agony, no one witnessed the rapid devastation of my once athletic body. As my physical capabilities diminished, I became aware that I would eventually need someone to assist me with the basic functions of living whenever that time came, and it was coming fast. It wouldn't be long before I would be completely paralyzed and permanently numbed on opiates. The signs were all around me. The famous commercial with the catch phrase, "I've fallen and I can't get up" no longer amused me. The news teemed with stories of people my age dying. The beggar outside 7-11 changed his sign from "Jesus Loves You" to "The End is Near."

I talked about death with anyone who would listen and with many people who would rather not. I ordered things I didn't need online so I could chat with the FedEx and UPS guys. Eventually they stopped ringing the bell and left my packages on my doorstep, even the ones that required a signature. People are very uncomfortable around death. They don't even like the word. Instead of saying, "So-and-so died," they say, "He passed," or "She crossed over." My favorite is, "He's in a better place." Yeah, right. Then it hit me. "A better place?" Hmm. Could I make that happen?

The answer arrived the next morning while I was all doped up, trying to focus on MedTV in my least uncomfortable chair. Outside my window I noticed that the two bunnies my neighbor had purchased a couple of months earlier had become a mob of bunnies hopping all over the place. That's when it dawned on me; all rabbits have to do is look cute and fuck. What a life. I had my answer. I would transform myself from a pain-crippled, decaying man of 53, into a fuzzy-eared, ten-pound sex machine. For the first time in months I felt hope; my life had a purpose once again, albeit temporary.

Having a task with a goal instantly reduced my pain by half. I almost discarded my new idea as being a bit crazy, but I knew the pain would return if I relaxed, so I got to work. I began my quest by taking the bus to pet stores all over town. I made use of my sleepless nights by Googling scores of sites on spiritual magic. My research unearthed a wide variety of shamans I had never been aware of before. Native American medicine men were happy to visit my home and accept hefty donations to convince me to shape-shift into an elk. Equally expensive Sufi mystics spun me into states of universal awareness and connectivity to the goodness of mankind. They would only accept cash. Monastic Hindis silenced my mind and revealed to me the solemn, powerful depths of eternal emptiness, which, by that time, matched the state of my wallet. I knew in my heart that there had to be a way to accomplish my dream, but I was growing weary of the spiritual scam artists who apparently reside in my woodwork. At last, I discovered the Tarahumara Indians from Barranca del Cobre, Mexico. I found their sacred text, The Way of The Beast, in the local library, translated into English. I contacted the publisher who put me in touch with the Shamans who authored the book. They really knew their stuff, willingly instructing me in the craft of soul transmutation through what they called the Copper Canyon peyote ritual. They required only their expenses and no extra fees. Their generosity convinced me. I think they also wanted to help so they could watch a gringo get stoked on magic mushroom sauce. These lessons added up to a surprisingly simple answer for me: you can spend all the money you want, but success boils down to Science of Mind. My father told me that when I was a kid—any problem in the universe can be solved by an unshakable belief in the principle of mind over matter, a powerful will, and perfect timing. I spent days, weeks with the Copper Canyon shamans. I studied and meditated and practiced. I was finally prepared. My short dark teachers saluted me and went back to Mexico, satisfied I would be able to transfer my spirit into another living being at the exact moment of my death.

To cover all my bets and be certain I was making the right choice, I considered other animals. I did not want to be any kind of wild animal, that's for sure. As beautiful as that life seemed in documentaries, the bottom line is they spend 24 hours a day on high alert for predators from up the food chain. Domestication was definitely the way to go. I considered various options. I didn't want to spend eternity eating seeds and running inside a plastic wheel, so rodents were out of the question. Dogs are loyal and loveable, but they sleep all the time, not the way I want to spend my extended life. Transmuting my soul into a horse would give me a nice long life, but the odds of finding a stud farm in Culver City, California were slim at best. Cats are loners, a trait I've always admired, but I wanted a change. I was tired of being alone. I wanted company. I want sex. I want to be a rabbit.

I prepared a list of post-transformation instructions, so my animal loving friends could look after me in my next life. I purchased strong wire cages to protect me from coyotes and hawks and I arranged for plenty of money in a trust to keep me supplied with organic carrots, lettuce and fluffy girl bunnies.

The final piece of the puzzle was choosing the perfect rabbit for my final incarnation; he must be young, have a strong sex drive and really big feet. I realized female rabbits will mate with just about any furry thing within reach, but four failed marriages, acute pain, and physical decay had sapped my self-confidence. I needed to insure my next life would be exactly what I wanted. Time was running out. Finally, at a pet store in El Segundo, I lucked upon a young, healthy, handsome male bunny with a lengthy pedigree of paternity and very large feet.

I am now ready to cross over. I feel confident that when the four-year life span of my next incarnation ends, I will die happy and satisfied, leaving behind a legacy of thousands of the cutest lettuce-munchers you ever saw.

Up yours, Death.

The Road to Pyrus

I slowly, blindly lowered myself off the bed and crawled across the wood floor like a hungover commando through masses of enemy bacteria and fungi to the bathroom. I sat on the toilet sideways and flushed my sticky eyelids with warm water while my addled brain shuffled through blurry mental images from the previous night. I vaguely remembered opening a Cabernet. I recalled *haricots verts* stir-frying in a saucepan by skinny arms decorated with silver bangles. That would be sweet Natalie Wilson, my assistant. I smiled at the memory of Natalie's youthful laughter, her short, yellow cotton sundress and sequin-covered ballet slippers. My reverie was interrupted by a soft, gurgling sound coming from the kitchen, accompanied by the sweet morning aroma of Kenya coffee. She must have set the automatic coffee maker. How embarrassing. Natalie had kindly volunteered to make me dinner in an attempt to civilize the slum my little cottage had become, and I expressed my gratitude by getting pie-eyed long before she arrived and passing out, I assume, during dinner. To top it off, she'd apparently undressed me and put me to bed. I'm sorry I missed that. I popped open a beer and swore never to drink again.

In these times of diminished recuperative powers and waning influence at the university, Natalie had remained my lone disciple, a former writing student who admired me far beyond what I deserved. She'd stuck around after graduation and had been working part time for me almost a year. Although her physical charms had a moving effect on the masculine me, her guileless nature and proficiency as an assistant forced me to maintain a professional posture. Who am I kidding? Natalie would never go for me. The only women who lusted my way anymore were middle-aged divorcées starting their second careers who'd already plowed through the younger versions of me. Undaunted by continual failure, I continued to chat up coeds night after night at campus hangouts, fortifying my waning sex appeal with volumes of draft beer. I'd even begun surfing the Internet for company and, yes, sometimes just for sex.

This pathetic phase of my life had begun a month earlier when Angela, my third wife, left me, citing a dehumanizing lack of attention to her needs and our 'incompatible emotional baggage.' I hate people who speak that way. Why couldn't she get angry drunk and smash crockery like a real woman?

I should be accustomed to women walking out on me by now. As Angela's van pulled away, I had a fleeting notion to use her rejection as an incentive to change my ways, perhaps to revise my nihilistic worldview, maybe give up fast food or go back to shaving every day. Instead, I added bourbon to my breakfast and stepped up my skirt-chasing. I ignored messages and emails, and left piles of uncorrected papers for Natalie to figure out. Except for robotic attendance at my classes, I hardly left my cramped, rundown house, which now, minus Angela, seemed oddly spacious and, dare I admit? - lonely.

The same day Angela left, the Dean warned me that my position with the university was in jeopardy. I responded by buying a huge flat screen TV and re-hanging my German expressionist art that Angela complained was 'narcissistic and gloomy.' By the way, it's entirely her fault that I'm a narcissist. If she had paid me a reasonable amount of attention, I wouldn't need to focus so much on myself.

* * * * *

Natalie didn't show up for work the rest of the week. It was not like her to not show up without calling. I was concerned but I let the time slide by because I was hardly looking forward to facing her after my humiliating bender. About a week later, I spent the night emotionally wrapped up in a "Law & Order" cable marathon and I forgot to drink. By morning, the bends of alcohol withdrawal had crippled all my major organs, apparently including my brain, because at precisely noon of that anxious, sweaty day, I rashly chose to parry the university's threat to abort my career. I typed a terse, bitter letter of resignation, and declared myself, to myself, a full time writer.

Sitting at my desk in silence staring at my resignation, I suddenly sensed that something had shifted within me, as though a tiny band of revolutionary cells in a corner of my mind had chosen a new path without consulting the rest of me. My vegan/yogi friend Malcolm called it a spiritual awakening. I call it an out-of-alcohol experience. I wasn't sure what it meant, but one thing was intuitively clear – I needed to do something to get out of myself. The mystery of Natalie's absence immediately came to mind.

She'd been working for me two days a week for over a year and never missed a day without an explanation—not to mention I owed her some back pay. I took my first shower in three days and drove two miles to her apartment, a four-story brick building in the working-class part of town. I parked my Austin-Healey roadster down the block so it wouldn't be obvious that I was there to see her. I don't know why I do things like that, like I was a detective or spy or whatever. Too much procedural TV? It's not like I cared what the university thought anymore. Probably just an old habit from sneaking around on women.

No one answered my knocking, so I took a chance and forced open the flimsy door. All the stuff that belongs in an apartment was still there and all the stuff that belongs to a person was missing, except for two pairs of shoes, a sure sign of a woman who left in a hurry. I looked everywhere. There were no clues to Natalie's whereabouts – no phone numbers scrawled in haste, no mail, nothing. The ashtray contained several Marlboro Lights, Natalie's brand, with lipstick on them, and one regular Marlboro with no lipstick. The only sign of a struggle, as TV detectives call it, was a wine glass with lipstick on the rim lying on the floor next to the coffee table. When I bent down to pick up the glass, I spotted a pair of black, size one panties under the coffee table. Had Natalie been raped? Kidnapped? Wait a minute. Was I overreacting? Maybe she simply ran off with a skinny lesbian. Time for more detective work.

The women in the Registrar's Office looked down their sober noses at my reputation, but since I hadn't yet been fired and my resignation letter sat impotent on my desk, they were still obliged to assist me. Natalie's file revealed she'd been a scholarship student, and her next of kin was listed as her mother, a Mrs. Wilson (no first name), whose only address was a post office box in a small town about a hundred miles away called Pyrus. That sounded familiar for some reason. I withdrew two hundred dollars at the ATM, splurged on high-octane gas for my roadster, and headed north.

The road to Pyrus is a two-lane blacktop far from the interstate highway system, a narrow ribbon of tar weaving along and around the drumlins that describe the glacially formed geography of the region. The countryside was dotted with grey, weathered barns and scattered herds of milk cows. Maples of every shade decorated the landscape while farther off, tall balsam firs guarded the base of low mountains. Purple, gold and red amaranth scented and brightened the roadside. I drove with the windows open to enjoy the aromas of rural earth and upstate flora.

Pyrus was the very definition of a small town with only one block of commerce. The only local eatery, Jerry's Diner, wasn't busy in mid-afternoon, so I took an unobtrusive seat in a corner booth and ordered coffee and pie. I passed the time by reading the history of the place on the back of the laminated menu, fanciful prose describing the owner's rod and reel triumphs in the Finger Lakes, alleged examples of which were mounted on the walls. My theory for finding Angela was, if I sat there long enough something would come to me; not much of a plan, but all I could think of at the time. After all, I'm not a real detective, I just watch them on TV.

I leafed through a discarded *Syracuse Post-Standard* and nursed countless cups of coffee while I watched customers traipse in and out under the gray-white fluorescent lighting, none of whom shook anything loose in my brain. They were mostly men clad in purposeful clothing who ordered food to go. A few gave me cursory glances and made comments to Joanne, the waitress/cashier. Joanne didn't look anything like Natalie. She was tall, with wide hips and a low center of gravity. Her Irish red hair was topped by a nurse-like cap secured by an arsenal of bobby pins. She didn't mind refilling my coffee and reiterating the variety of pies every time I asked. I wanted to ask her about Natalie, but I felt out of my depth nosing around a country berg for a young girl. People in small towns are private by nature and a middle-aged man asking questions about a twenty-something female would raise their hackles quickly. I imagined the worst—some deranged cousin or protective neighbor overhearing my inquiries and flexing his provincial loyalty by taking a baseball bat to my beautiful British car.

Having enjoyed the apple, cherry and blueberry pies, I was about to sample the peach cobbler (they didn't serve alcohol) when I heard Joanne shout to Jerry in the kitchen that she was going to pick up the mail before it got too busy. Hello! I had what I call an idiot idea. That's when you realize something so obvious that you wonder why you didn't think of it a lot sooner. Natalie's only address in the college records had been a post office box, yet it hadn't occurred to me to check out the post office! I stalled a minute to avoid running into Joanne, then slid across the yellow vinyl bench seat, careful to avoid the busted tuft button that could tear a giant hole in the pants of a less cautious man. I left a relatively hefty 'thank you for letting me sit a spell' tip and headed in Joanne's direction, but on the other side of the street, searching for an American flag.

The sky had turned overcast and a chill swept along Main Street. The so-called post office at the other end of the block turned out to be an alcove in the rear of a combination pharmacy, dry goods, and arts & crafts store. I pretended to look in the window of a ladies' clothing shop until I saw Joanne head back to the diner. I crossed the street. More fluorescent lighting. One woman ran the entire place. Her name was Katherine, "Call me Kate," Underwood. She was a registered pharmacist and a champion knitter, specializing in alpaca boatneck sweaters. The walls of her establishment were lined with basketball trophies and blue ribbons she had won at knitting bees, a popular amusement in this part of the state. She had athletic shoulders and social energy. Her blond hair was cut short, no doubt to prevent tangling with yarn, and her sharp blue eyes surveyed her retail domain from a perch behind a counter near the front door. I liked her right away, but women my age never appeal to me – even smart, attractive ones like Kate. My fellow academics used to offer to introduce me to fortyish women, but I always made excuses, preferring to ply my father-figure charm on college girls.

Kate Underwood had a straightforward way about her, so I took a chance she might appreciate that quality in others and told her what I was looking for. I left out the part about getting drunk and Natalie putting me to bed. Those omissions notwithstanding, Kate accepted the avuncular nature of my concern and willingly headed for the U. S. government section of her store.

The P. O. box in question was overstuffed with mail, which Kate began sorting through. She wouldn't go so far as to let me handle the mail, but she did allow me to look over her shoulder, explaining to me, perhaps for legal purposes, that she periodically rearranged crowded mailboxes for the benefit of the postal customer. Thank God for small towns. Those kinds of shenanigans in a major city would surely be a felony. Among the junk mail and university correspondences, there was one blue envelope addressed to N. James, possibly Natalie's alias. The scrawled return address said, "R. S., 363 DeWitt Street, Cloverfield," another small town halfway between Pyrus and the university. Kate held that envelope steady long enough for me to jot the address on a matchbook. Suddenly, I felt scared—my next move might put me in direct confrontation with Natalie's abductor. Playing passive-pretend-detective was one thing, actually rescuing her from a homicidal kidnapper was something else altogether.

"Excuse me, Kate, do you sell beer?" The least I could do was spend a few bucks in her store.

I sat in my car outside Jerry's drinking cold Utica Clubs, smoking Camel Lights, searching for a non-country radio station, and wondering what in the world had compelled me to drive a hundred miles upstate. Natalie was probably lying on a beach in Florida without a care. She probably came to her senses that awful night, and realized she was wasting her young life covering for a brilliant, charming drunk. She didn't owe me any explanations.

It began to rain. My knees throb when it rains. My wipers weren't working too well either, streaking my side of the windshield with a rainbow of brown arcs. British cars of a certain era received high marks for style, yet they were notoriously faulty in wet weather. You would think a car designed and built in England would not suffer wipers that streak, windows that leak, and lights that fail in the rain, wouldn't you?

I sat there, unable to get those black panties out of my mind, unable to make a decision, when the bloat of three beers and rain sluicing down all four sides of my car made me suddenly desperate for urinary relief. I pulled my jacket over my head and ran into the diner, heading straight for the men's room. I nodded to Joanne's replacement on the way and she smiled back at me. She had small teeth.

I stood at the *pissoir* checking out the local graffiti and enjoying the minor existential rapture of emptying a bloated bladder, when it occurred to me that the new waitress looked familiar. I was washing my hands, annoyed by the yellow evidence of my Camel addiction on my left index finger, when the recesses of my memory burst open. The woman at the counter was an older version of a one-night stand I had picked up near closing time at a campus sports bar twenty-some years earlier! How could I forget — she had the most talented lips ever to visit my nether regions and she mentioned she was from Pyrus, which seemed odd at the time. She lived 100 miles from the bar, yet agreed to come to my place in a wink. By the time we arrived at my apartment, I was too drunk to make the effort. She just smiled and proceeded to become my private Sherpa, guiding me to the peak of Mt. Pleasure. I remember thinking, as her mouth performed its miracle, that I hoped one day to marry a woman with this much skill and generosity. When I woke up the next morning she was gone. Her Lone Ranger disappearing act didn't bother me because I had a girlfriend at the time and Pyrus seemed so far away. I might have followed up on her for a reprise of our blissful night together, but she never gave me her number or told me her name.

And now, twenty-odd years later, I was pretty sure that she was working the counter at Jerry's diner in Pyrus, New York. I decided to detour from the Natalie mystery and indulge my nostalgic curiosity. The restroom was poorly lit and its mirror was scratched, saving me from the sight of what two decades of debauchery had done to my boyish good looks. My teeth looked clean but my breath was probably woeful from the mixture of coffee, beer, cigarettes and three kinds of pie. I accepted the verdict of my reflection, took a very deep breath and walked out the door and into my past.

The object of my curiosity was cashing out a customer, so I slipped a free peppermint under my tongue and watched. She was still in good shape and her high heels, though impractical for waitress work, flattered her legs. Her skirt was short and her ring finger was empty. I was looking at the first woman over forty that had ever turned me on. I guess it helped that we had some history together.

I perched on a stool at the counter and asked her for coffee. The badge on her blouse said, "Nancy," but that name didn't ring a bell. Business had picked up and kept her moving constantly. She performed her job efficiently and with a smile, showing no signs of recognizing me. Joanne returned and quickly jumped in to share the work. When I asked for a refill, Nancy rested for a minute.

"You're pretty busy here tonight." I turned to face her.

"It's always busy on Wednesdays, who knows why. And the regular girl is sick, so Joanne asked me to help out. Then Joanne's babysitter freaked out, said her son was bleeding to death or something."

It always amazed me how small town people will chat with just about anyone. "Really? Is he all right?"

"All right? That rascal makes Dennis the Menace look like a choirboy. He got hold of some fake blood to scare the crap out of the sitter." She laughed.

"I bet Joanne didn't think it was funny."

"Oh, not to worry. Little Miss Clueless had it coming. She's like one of those Mean Girls you see on TV. She was watching music videos, totally ignoring her job, when Caleb staggered in like he'd hurt himself, with blood all over his face. The bimbo saw him and screamed, 'Oh my God, oh my God!'"

Nancy practically choked with laughter telling me this story.

"Then the kid lurched forward and gurgled fake blood out of his mouth and all over her."

I waited for her to come down from her giddy paroxysms.

"You have any kids of your own?"

"Yeah, I have a daughter, but she's not a kid anymore. She's a college graduate. First one in our family."

"Good for her. You must be proud."

"I suppose."

"What do you mean?"

"Well, number one, she's a living reminder of her long gone, pothead father, and number two, she isn't doing anything with her education."

"Sometimes college kids take a while to figure out what they want."

She took in my comment in with a smirk. "I can see you never had kids."

Just then someone summoned her down the counter. If she had recognized me she didn't let on. Perhaps our night together hadn't been quite as memorable for her. I wondered how long I would carry on this game.

I sipped my coffee and drifted off into daydreams about the night we met, when she renewed the conversation. "You're not from around here, are you?"

"Uh, no, I'm on my way upstate, just thought I'd stop here for a coffee."

"Is that so?"

"Yeah, just passing through, as they say."

She planted one hand on her hip and stared me down. "I don't know what you're up to, mister, but Joanne told me you were sitting in the corner booth earlier today for a couple of hours, and I don't cotton to liars."

She looked directly into my eyes during the silence that followed. I was embarrassed, but there's something irresistible about her candor. I still wasn't absolutely sure she was the one from my past, so I told a partial truth.

"Okay. Actually, I'm looking for someone who's from here."

"What are you, some kind of private eye or something?"

I had to laugh at that romantic notion.

"Hardly." I figured I had nothing to lose at this point. "Seriously, my assistant hasn't shown up for work for over a week and she's originally from Pyrus, so I came looking for her."

"Why didn't you call the cops?"

"I don't know. I guess I thought they wouldn't believe me. I'm not related to her or anything. I just wanted to find out why she vanished without a word. It's not like her."

Our conversation was rudely interrupted by Jerry's bark from the kitchen, "Patty, pickup for table seven."

"I got work to do. Good luck to you, mister. I hope your friend's okay." She balanced three meat loaf specials on her right arm, grabbed the coffee pot with her left hand, and was swallowed up by the swarm of life in the diner. As I watched her walk away, my eyes slipped out of focus and I recalled our first meeting, her coat with the fur-lined hood, her doe-brown eyes, our brief but splendid evening of pleasure two decades previous.

It suddenly hit me. Jerry just called her Patty, but her badge said Nancy. It doesn't really matter because she didn't recognize me and I didn't remember either name. Okay. That's enough. Detour over. Time to find Natalie.

I asked Joanne for a coffee to go and left without saying goodbye to Nancy/Patty. I drove cautiously through the rain all the way to Cloverfield, wary of being slightly over the legal limit from the three beers and the likelihood that one of my lights could go out at any time and draw the attention of a bored state trooper.

It was dark by the time I reached Cloverfield. My weary bones wanted to continue south to my cozy, messy cottage, finish those Uticas and start my life over the next day, but something compelled me to complete my quest. I pulled into a gas station to ask directions and it turned out the address I had scribbled down was right around the corner.

I felt scared again. I was dying to know that Natalie was okay, but at that point, I just wanted this wild-goose chase to be over with. The truth was, I really didn't know much about her. I questioned my motives to have undertaken this investigation, like I was acting out of turn, minding someone else's business—I guess part of me wanted to feel like a kind of hero.

I parked the car and walked up a narrow path to a one-story cabin even smaller than my humble digs but with a wide porch in front, complete with a swinging loveseat. The porch light was on and I thought I heard a television. I took a deep breath and knocked. Natalie came to the door, wearing sweatpants and a college t-shirt.

"Professor Dawkins!"

"Hi, Natalie." She looked tired but happy. I was confused.

"How did you find me? Are you all right?"

I felt like an idiot. All this drama and driving all over the bloody countryside, and there she was, perfectly fine.

"Who is it, Nat?" A man's voice rang out from inside the house. *Uh-oh.* That made me nervous.

She turned and semi-shouted over her shoulder, "It's my boss."

'My boss.' That cemented the generation gap between us. "I'm sorry to bother you. I just... I hadn't heard from you since that night, you know..."

I literally hung my head. I was suffering a repeat of the humiliation of having to be put to bed by this girl who had not signed up for that job.

"It's okay, sir. Actually, I'm flattered you went to all this trouble."

"So, you're okay? You're not being held captive against your will?"

She laughed. My question was half serious, but I was relieved she found it funny.

"Would you like to meet him? Come on in." She shouted over her shoulder again, "Rafe, put your shirt on and c'mere."

Their house was tiny and bare. From the small, dimly lit hallway I could see the outline of a sofa in the glow of a TV. A handsome, wiry boy with a mop of thick black hair came into the entry hall as he buttoned his shirt. Natalie stood next to him, grabbed his arm with both her hands, and tilted her head against his shoulder. They both had that dreamy look of young lovers in the throes.

"This is my boyfriend, Rafael."

"Hi, Mr. Dawkins. I've heard a lot about you from Nat."

"Please, call me Jay."

"He just got out of jail a week ago. I've been waiting for him for three years."

Well, I'd been right about one thing. He was a felon. Aside from their obvious near-poverty and a crude tattoo of the crucifixion partially visible on his pectoral muscle, he seemed fairly civilized. The would-be crime scene back at

Natalie's apartment made sense now. Every muscle in my body finally relaxed with relief and exhaustion.

"Well, it's good to know you're all right." I shook Rafael's hand goodbye. "Nice to meet you. Take good care of her."

"No problem, sir." He went back to the TV, and Natalie walked me out onto the porch.

"I'm sorry I didn't call or anything. The combination of that night and Rafe getting out kinda spun my head around. All I could think of was being with him."

"I'm the one who should apologize."

"Don't worry about it." She smiled up at me. No wonder he was in love with her. I reached into my pocket, took out all the bills and pushed them into her hand.

"I brought your back pay." They needed the money a lot more than I did, and they were more deserving, that's for sure.

"Thank you." She held onto my hand, leaned into me and whispered in my ear.

"Don't tell mom about Rafe."

"What? What do you mean?"

"She doesn't know that I'm with him. She doesn't approve."

"But... I don't know your mother."

"Yes, you do. She called me on my cell a little while ago and said some man was up in Pyrus looking for me. When she described him, I knew it was you right away. I was going to call you in the morning."

Then it hit me – shiny dark hair, small teeth, and a sweet smile with a touch of melancholy. It all made sense now. Of course her mother wouldn't tell me anything. I could have been a sociopath rapist stalking her daughter. The hairs on the back of my neck were bristling like tall grass in the wind, each follicle raised off the surface by the alarming, happy news that serendipity exists. Natalie was looking at me, quizzically.

"Don't worry. I won't say a word."

"Thanks."

"Well, that's it. Bye for now. Thanks again for all your help."

"Bye, Professor." She breathed a smile and closed the door. I can imagine how quickly she returned to the arms of her lover. That Rafael was one lucky parolee.

I was beat. I longed for the depths of dreamland, already feeling the relief of my familiar bed beneath me. As I drove south, my mind drifted through memories of a young Patty in the bar in her fur-lined parka, then sitting naked on my bed, her feet tucked under her beautiful ass, grinning down at me like a girl happy to be alive. Like in a dream, my mind shifted to the present, to the older Patty in her short waitress skirt, her brown hair longer but still shiny, the sparkle in her eyes still inviting. I pulled over to the side of the road and sat there with the engine running in the middle of nowhere. My mind was blank and racing. I checked out my face in the rear-view mirror and saw the familiar look of confusion and low-grade anxiety. I thought about Natalie with her head resting lovingly on Rafael's shoulder and I wanted that feeling.

The rain had stopped but the streets were still slick and shiny, reflecting the lights of the cars and trucks that whizzed past my idling roadster in the night, their drivers unaware of the shift in my heart. I flicked on my blinker, swung a u-turn and headed back to Pyrus.

Miracles

My great aunt Armena loves to tell stories. She sits in the same corner booth she's occupied since God knows when, and sips her tea, nowadays with one artificial sweetener rather than the sugar cube the doc suggested might not be so good for her. She sips lightly, careful not to spill a drop on the turquoise retro eyeglasses hanging from a jeweled chain around her neck. She hasn't changed her hairstyle since I've known her, parted on the left side, with a tortoise shell barrette with three tiny plastic daisies on it. When she talks she tilts her head to one side, like a person saying "awww" at the sight of a cute puppy.

Armena and her late husband, Hank Willis, grew up right here in Crumford, a quiet little hamlet whose only resource was the uneven tourist business from visitors to the medium-sized lake on the northern edge of town. Hank was elected Sherriff a record 17 times before he willingly retired, and Armena used to work in his office at the switchboard back in the 60s and 70s, so she has plenty of stories to tell. Her favorite tale was about a boy named Roy Crittendon who became a local legend decades ago by what Armena liked to call 'whipping up a hullabaloo of mayhem.' She always begins her favorite story with the same words: "Rambunctious was about the kindest word anyone ever used to describe young Roy."

For several years back in the old days, this legendary wild child was the primary topic of conversation among the regulars who frequented Mabel's Restaurant, owned and operated by Armena's cousin, and the only eating establishment in town not primarily catering to the lake crowd. At exactly three fifteen every afternoon, Armena turned the switchboard over to whichever young deputy was on duty, and walked one block to Mabel's for her daily gossip fix. When her friends spotted Armena strutting down the street in her Deputy uniform, everyone scooted around the big circular booth to make room for her. She claimed she didn't approve of gossip, but being the *de facto* hub of Crumford's communication system, her arrival at Mabel's was the high point of the day for the gang in the corner. Armena made a point of never telling them the latest news until she had taken her seat and Mabel had poured her a cup of tea to which she methodically added one sugar cube.

Back in those days, the conversation was most frequently focused on Roy, the town terror. Aunt Armena's crowd at the corner table had strong opinions of a similar stripe:

'I heard he cut the tail off of poor Marilyn Sankey's old dog.'

'My girls are scared to walk anywhere nowadays, day or night.'

'I've been telling y'all for years, he's just plain crazy.'

'Crazy is one thing, but that boy's dangerous.'

Eighty-year-old Frederick Masters always sat directly to Armena's left, from whence he daily repeated his more thoughtful theory that Roy's wild streak was the result of his family's misfortune, pinpointing the onset of Roy's fractured temperament to the day that Roy's father lost three-quarters of his right leg in an accident at the Crow's Point textile mill, which forced the family to go on disability.

"'They had to move to a tiny place south of Elm, remember? The two boys had to share a bedroom.'

Mrs. Threadkill was quick to point out that plenty of people had it worse than Roy. 'I shared a room with my two sisters 'til I was sixteen. You don't see me going around beating up on people and smashing stuff.'

'Oh, come on now, 'Risa, you know girls aren't prone to violence. I'm sorry, but that's just not a good example.'

'Oh, is that so, Mr. Smartypants? What about Bonnie what's-her-name, the bank robber? What about your cousin over in Dual Forks who set her momma's house on fire?'

'Bonnie wouldn't have been Bonnie without Clyde, and everyone knows my cousin had certified brain damage.'

'Well, maybe Roy was dropped on *his* head.'

Frederick rolled his eyes as Mabel stopped by to refill the coffee cups. She liked to chime in too, now and then.

'Y'all still trying to figure out what flipped Roy's switch? Lemme tell you, things just happen, you know, with no rhyme or reason anywhere in sight. God knows I appreciate you're having these discussions on my watch, but let's face it, that boy was born a miniature monster and that's all there is to that.'

'But you can't deny,' chimed in Frederick once again, 'that Roy's personality disorder coincided with his daddy's accident, now can you?'

Joanne Fogerty stopped fiddling with her napkin. 'Personality disorder? I declare, you're starting to sound like that Phil Donahue feller on the television.'

Mabel waited her turn to respond to the self-appointed brainiac, aiming her retort directly to Masters, 'Let me ask you something, Mr. Mensa. When I get out of bed at 6:30 in the morning, and the sun comes up right after, does that make me responsible for the daylight?'

Everybody laughed uproariously, as though they hadn't heard this argument a thousand times.

'Say what you want. Everybody knows that boy turned rotten when his family fell on hard times, and it's been downhill ever since.' Masters liked to have the last word. But as Mabel headed back toward the kitchen, we all heard her mumble, 'I wonder if anybody ever dropped you on *your* head.' The titters around the table went unnoticed by Frederick, who was busy stewing as Mabel walked away, that same feeling he had felt for decades, a feeling that everyone knew about but no mentioned - a deep, abiding, and unspoken adoration of Mabel.

"Truth be told," Armena continued, "Frederick Masters had a point. Roy did not begin beating up his older brother, Ned, Jr., on a regular basis until they moved to the south side after the accident. Everybody in town knew that Roy was terrorizing his brother, but Crumford was the kind of town where we minded their own business and preferred to let families work out their own problems. No father or mother likes to be told how to raise their young'ns, which works out just fine until the family's business becomes the town's business. A year or so after the Crittendons moved to the south side Roy's violence began to spread outside his family. He started picking fights in school and knocking over trash cans and mailboxes on the way home. By age ten, Roy had punched up dozens of boys, stolen from stores and houses, frightened girls of all ages and damaged a considerable amount of public and private property. A host of unsolved misdemeanors and vandalisms were attributed to the miniature menace. Most people suspected it was Roy who set the fire at the post office that summer but no one could prove it. People complained to one another and to my Hank, but no one had any idea what to do about that boy."

One Wednesday afternoon Armena received a call that summoned Sherriff Willis to the playground of the regional school.

"It seems Roy had smashed a open-end wrench across the skull of the school bully, Joseph Connor, and knocked him cold. The hospital in nearby Abbottsville said the gash in young Connor's head required nineteen stitches. Roy didn't even try to get away. Sherriff Hank later told me that when he arrived, the boy was quietly standing over his victim, with the bloody wrench in his hand. He looked up at Hank, dropped the wrench, and calmly offered his wrists for the handcuffs. Like he'd had a moment of regret or he wanted to get caught. It sounded eerie to me."

While Roy was in custody for the alleged assault, Armena got a close up look at him in the holding cell as they waited for the juvenile authorities to arrive. She couldn't wait to repeat her observations to the gang at Mabel's.

"'First off,' she said, 'He's not your typical criminal type, if you know what I mean. He doesn't have an Alfred E. Neuman face or anything.'

Joanne Fogerty couldn't sit still, she was so excited about the prospect of hearing first hand information. 'Is he fidgety? They say serial killers and career criminals are fidgety.'

Armena admitted she couldn't fuel their fire. 'Nope. He doesn't drool or talk to himself or use profanity. And you're not going to believe this, but when Hank made him wash up and slick his hair down, I swear, he looked like a perfectly normal boy any family would be proud of.'

Mabel chipped in again, 'I remember seeing him in church when he was little. He had a good singing voice, as I recall.'

'That's right. I remember. He had good posture, too.'

'And kids loved playing with him. Our little Jimmy was over there every day before they moved.'

'Not to mention, he gets straight-A's in school.'

'Boy, am I sick of hearing about that.'

'If it wasn't for his grades and that meddling Bernice Delacroix, he'd be rotting in Juvenile Hall where he belongs.'

'As if that nosy social worker knows anything.'

'So what if he makes A's. Tell that to Marilyn Sankey's dog.'

'Between Delacroix and those old Baptist bitties coming to his defense, you'd think it was *our* fault he turned out to be the devil himself. They're always claiming he was some kind of savant or whatever.'

'The kids at school are saying there's no trouble anymore, what with Roy settin' in jail and Joe Connor havin' learnt his lesson.

'I suppose that's something.'

'We'll see how long that lasts. You can't fix something that's broke that bad.'

Everybody except Frederick Masters said, 'Amen.'"

After the Joe Conner/wrench incident, Roy was given yet another reprieve by the powers that be, and the population of Crumford was once again advised to lock their doors, keep their pets inside and make sure they knew the whereabouts of their children at all times. Then, on his eleventh birthday, in the clear view of several witnesses, Roy threw a brick at the windshield of a passing Greyhound bus, causing the Regional Youth Authority to finally overrule Ms. Delacroix and the Bible thumpers. A clear-minded judge promptly sent him off to a state detention center for a year.

A big smile always spread across Armena's face at this point in the story. She would tilt her head to the opposite side, take a sip of tea and ask me if I minded if she partook of some biscuits. I would always say, "Please, ma'am, you go right ahead."

She smiled and settled in for part two of the story.

"With Roy locked up, you'd think the citizens were all on permanent summer vacation. Everyone leisurely lolled about, knowing Roy wouldn't be strangling their pets or slashing the contents of their clotheslines to ribbons. They went back to leaving their doors unlocked and letting their children play in the woods."

Sherriff Willis's switchboard was so quiet, he and Armena actually took a short vacation. They drove down to Charleston to visit his maiden aunt Sylvia and her life companion Louise P. Heinrich.

Crumford's holiday of relief and contentment ended abruptly when Roy was released two months before his sentence was up, "for 'good behavior' if you can believe that." He was dropped off in town by the state Juvenile Department of Corrections, at which time he immediately proceeded to beat up his brother Ned for the ten millionth time.

The next day's round table discussion centered around the possibility that the town was hexed, that maybe their suffering was karmic punishment for some moral crime committed by their forefathers. It wouldn't be the first time a town was the victim of an ages-old curse, but Crumford had no history of natural disasters normally associated with hexed villages such as lightning strikes, tornadoes or other unnatural occurrences.

Frederick chimed in with the answer to the unspoken question on everyone's mind: 'No,' he said, 'no one in Crumford ever owned slaves. I'd like to say it was a moral choice, but the simple truth is, no one could afford to.'

Roy's second reign of havoc lasted almost three months. Day after day people found damage on their property or one of their kids would come home with a black eye or stolen lunch money. Just when the entire population was simultaneously getting ready to officially insist the Sherriff do something about Roy, there was a lull. Things got real quiet. There was no vandalism, no dogs barking, nothing missing for an entire week. Then the news broke.

Armena was the first to hear, of course, and couldn't wait to get over to Mabel's. She left her post immediately, unable to resist the urge to share the biggest piece of information in the modern history of Crumford. As she so aptly put it, "No decent, God-fearing Christian would ever own up to it out loud, but every man, woman, and child in town, (minus Roy's family, of course—and we weren't sure about them), heaved a sigh of relief the day that Roy turned up dead in Connor's Woods."

And that's not half of what makes this story worth repeating. What turned this tale of a wild child into a local legend, was an act of providence of cosmic proportion. The week that Roy's body was discovered coincided with what became known as 'The Miracle of Connors Woods,' the oddest event in the 200-year-old history of Crumford. A few days before Roy's body was discovered, right after a typical summer afternoon thunderstorm, a large hunk of rock oozed up out of the ground in the middle of Connor's woods. It was shaped like the nose cone on a moon rocket, about as big as a decent-sized tool shed, and there was no explanation for it whatsoever. It was truly a miracle.

The next thing anyone knew, Crumford was flooded with spiritual seekers from far and wide. The townsfolk were used to summer people coming to spend time at the lake, but this was an altogether different crowd. Many wore flowing robes and headbands with precious amulets around their necks. The rest of them were old-fashioned religious types, the Pentacostals and Witnesses and Born-Agains, all hoping to glean some spiritual wisdom from this miracle of nature.

The stone was, according to Frederick Masters, 'not constituted of any geological material normally found in the area. It was several shades of gray with flecks of white, with that stratified look of parallel lines along its sides. It was about six feet high and sort of pointed, but not sharp like an arrow, more like a pointy igloo, or the front end of a small-sized jet airplane. It jutted out of the ground at about 45 degrees in the midst of a small clearing in the woods, and gave the impression that there was a lot more of it below ground than above, like an iceberg.'

Armena always laughed at this very same point in the story, because she always, always forgot to mention that the weather changed right about the time the stone appeared. The rock oozed out of the ground during a typical 30-minute summer thunderstorm but the next day it rained for four hours and continued pretty much every afternoon like that for several hours at a time until the whole county was soggy and muddy and chilled to the bone. The downpour was not the most important fact in the story, but it definitely added to the mystery of the coincidences.

It wasn't long before the protruding rock in the clearing quickly became a powerful magnet for lost souls, dreamers, evangelists, repentant sinners, and the simply curious from all over.

"Mabel had a theory about the pilgrims: 'You know, the further folks travel to see a 'miracle,' the more amazed they're likely to be, right? Think about it. If a sojourner puts in her effort, she's going to want commensurate results, right? Say you're sitting right here at your usual table, for example, and somebody says, 'Hey, don't that look just like Jesus over there on Winnie's Esso sign?' All you have to do is turn your head, look out the window, and say 'yes' or 'no' or 'oh, come on now.' No big deal, right? If it is or it ain't, it's no skin off your nose. You see what I'm getting at? So imagine, when you drive 500 miles in a pickup truck with bald tires on back roads to see some stone sticking out of the ground, then you better have one heck of an experience to justify all that gas money and your stiff back and everybody telling you you're out of your mind. Am I right or am I right?'" Armena shook her head from side to side and laughed at the happy memory of her dear cousin Mabel.

"It's a good thing your great uncle and I took that little trip to Charleston when we did, because pilgrims were arriving in droves from all over the tri-state area and even as far away as Athens, Greece to get a glimpse of what they all started calling 'Rockland County's geological miracle.' I declare. There were ten times as many of these spiritual travelers than even the summer lake crowd, which was diminished that year on account of the endless rain, the third factor in the summer of miracles. The entire town was muddier than a pigpen for several weeks.

"It's amazing how the visitors knew more about our town than we did. We didn't know, for example, that the Connor family, who had received the land as a grant from the British Crown, was originally descended from an ancient noble that had fallen from grace in the United Kingdom, not difficult for an Irishman, and all the Connors were exiled to the New World.

"Anyway, between the throngs of seekers clogging Dublin Road and the incessant rain, it took Hank and his two deputies a while to start looking into the circumstances of Roy's death. Meanwhile, rumors were born, embellished, mutated, and spread around the county faster than a flu epidemic. Everyone had an opinion, because everyone had a story about Roy. Every phone line was busy, every public place filled with chatter. Not much got done around Crumford for several days."

None of this anecdotal information advanced Hank's investigation, however. The authorities had precious little factual information. Ned, Jr. was the first person everyone thought of, but he and his parents had been at Mabel's enjoying her famous chicken fried steak at the official time of death, which was estimated by the Rockland County Coroner at six p.m., give or take. The unsuspecting Crittendons didn't even know until Armena arrived with the news. Their stunned reaction right away convinced her of their innocence. Having to tell the family about the death of their son was the most uncomfortable moment ever in Armena's professional life.

There was no evidence at the scene of any forensic value. Footprints that might have provided clues in the dank woods had been trampled over by the curious crowd of miracle-seekers or washed away by the rain. Rumor had it that the initial examination of the body indicated he had been beaten or choked, or both. Hank wisely called in the state police to assist. The crowd at Mabel's corner table was working the case in their own way.

"Someone said they heard Roy went to the woods to meet up with someone, but Armena knew from Hank that molestation has been eliminated as a theory of the crime.

'I can name dozens of people who'd like to molest him, just not in *that* way.'

'Besides, didn't that pervert - what's his name – Paul something? Didn't he go off to the Episcopalian Seminary last year?'

'Yes he did. And he swore he'd never come back.'

'Good riddance.'

Everyone at the table except Frederick Masters said, 'Amen.'

"Sheriff Hank asked for help to comb the area. The only requirement to join this homegrown posse was free time and a workable pair of boots. Frederick was the first person to volunteer. He jumped into the thick of it, hoping he'd be the one who crack the case open.

Utilizing his early police academy training, Hank organized systematic, thorough searches, fanning out in ever-widening circles from the crime scene but nothing was found. After a few days, when the initial buzz began to ebb, the question was raised one morning among the regulars at Mabel's as to whether the emergence of the Stone, this biblical rain, and the death of young Roy were connected. Jim Gibberly played substitute genius, since Frederick was out searching, pointing out the *post hoc, propter hoc* fallacy, a theory with which the round table was well-acquainted with in less formal terms from Mabel's oft-quoted sunrise example. It was generally accepted, however, that one did not have to be religiously persuadable to believe that some coincidences were odder than others.

Once again, the local phone lines were alive with gossip about what was now being called the *double* miracle." Armena rolled her eyes to the heavens, "It didn't take much."

"As word spread throughout the south, a reporter from Mobile, Alabama was dispatched to write a story about The Stone for his newspaper, which was owned and read mostly by evangelical Christians. None of us thought much about it, mind you, what with strangers everywhere you looked. This so-called journalist was a falsely cheerful type with beady eyes and ears that stuck out like flaps. He always dressed in a worn-out, black suit in spite of the weather, with pamphlets and scraps of paper sticking out of most of his pockets. His umbrella had one spike sticking out with no cloth on it so his left shoulder was always soaked through. His shoddy shoes were quickly ruined by the rain and mud. He interviewed lots of people, including me, along with Doctor Krohn and a couple of preachers. Sherriff Hank would never talk to the press during an ongoing open investigation. The article appeared a few days later and made frequent references to miracles, the devil, and the mystical power of prayer. The writer drew the conclusion, if you could call it that, that the rock had been sent by God to save the town from Roy." Armena rolled her eyes twice at that reference.

"Nobody in town paid any mind to that newspaper article, except that it led to the next part of the story. A TV station in Montgomery (not to be outdone by their rivals in Mobile) sent a full reporting crew up north to expand the story into a mini-documentary, which aired on their high-powered station as the lead story of the Sunday six-o'clock news. Suddenly, tens of thousands of people in seven states had heard about 'The Double Miracle of Rockland County.'"

The otherwise blasé population of Crumford couldn't resist tuning in to the broadcast. Mabel even brought in a tiny TV with collapsible rabbit ears from her daughter's room so the rumor squad could watch it together without leaving the psychological comfort of their corner table. The most effective and revealing interview was with a thoughtful young girl in glasses and a plain blue dress who revealed that she had been teaching Roy how to play the oboe. Now that there was an odd piece of information no one had expected. Anyone playing the oboe in the land of banjos and gut buckets was a bit of miracle in its own right.

This new aspect of Roy's story had every eye in Mabel's glued to the set as the camera zoomed in on little Maria, her dark hair pinned to her temple with a homemade ribbon. "Roy and I used to meet after school and practice together in the woods not far from my house. Just far enough so nobody would hear us. I would play a phrase and he would try and copy me. We took turns. It was fun."

"We all realized she must have been the last person to see Roy alive. She certainly was the only person in town who didn't seem to be afraid of him. She innocently deflected the religious inferences the reporter kept insisting were at the root of the event, and told her story in the softest, sweetest voice this side of Kansas, causing even the most skeptical to conclude she was telling the truth."

"Oh, I don't know about that," she quietly stated, "all I know is I accidentally discovered this caney sort of plant in the woods one day, and it seemed like the same kind of wood as the reeds my dad sends away to Richmond for."

Armena said it was the longest time she had ever seen that table full of chatterboxes at Mabel's sit still without talking. This little child musician had learned how fashion her own oboe reeds. Talk about miracles.

Maria continued, "I don't have any friends, really, so when I found the reed plant, I told Roy about it the next day at school because his desk was next to mine. He asked me if I would play something for him. So I met him after school several days in a row and played my lessons for him. Then one day he asked me to teach him how to play."

"I remember Jim Gibberly was practically in tears, staring at her little face on television.

And Martha knew Maria and her family from shopping at the general store and said, 'They're very honest people. They pay for things I didn't see them pick up and the little girl walked all the way back into town one day to pay a bill.'

"Mrs. Poole said, 'she's a good student, too. She keeps to herself, but a nice enough little girl.'"

Mabel said, 'You know, her story might explain why things were so quiet the week or so before Roy died, remember? It was probably because he was in the woods with Maria.'"

Other people who claimed to know of her said she was not given to lying, nor was she the lovesick type who might come to the defense of an outcast against all authority and common sense.

There was a moment when Maria's father, Frank, was on the TV screen. 'We were appalled at the idea of our only daughter being acquainted with the deceased, but we stand behind out talented little girl during these calamitous times.'

"Young Maria's unabashed sincerity in her television interview brought up guilt feelings and confusion in most people who had hated this poor dead boy who apparently had a soft side and even wanted to learn the oboe, of all things. That set the table abuzz.

'What are we supposed to think now?'

'Was Roy one of those mentally unbalanced children?'

'Are you saying it wasn't his fault?'

'What the heck do I know about psychology?'"

The townspeople didn't want to feel ignorant, which they weren't, but nevertheless, they began buying into the myriad of new-age theories that sprang up like mosquitoes in July, mostly proliferated by the outsiders who'd come to see The Stone.

Sherriff Willis, on the other hand, had no interest in theories. His only interest was in *facts*. The focus of his investigation came to roost on a select few citizens. Armena

kept her table of talkers informed of the latest dope:
Marylin Sankey had been in Atlanta the week of the crime
meeting with a veterinary surgeon, and the two teachers
who had received anonymous death threats were questioned
and released. Hank was logically interested in several
members of the old Connor family, particularly Patrick, the
father of the bully who Roy had conked with a wrench. The
Sherriff was very aware that every single Sunday since
Joseph's beating some member of this hard-drinking clan
swore revenge on Roy. This usually occurred moments
before the would-be avenger stumbled off a barstool and
knocked himself unconscious. To hear Armena tell it,
people avoided the Connors as they would keep clear of a
bull in a pasture during mating season. She said they were
unfit to socialize with decent folks, which was truly a
shame, because Asa Connor, the 18th century founder of
their town, was historically renowned as an honest and
industrious man who would undoubtedly turn in his grave if
he could see his descendants wasting the Lord's day
stinking up a roadhouse with empty oaths and whiskey-
fueled bravado.

Armena, with the infinite wisdom of hindsight,
pointed out one benefit that can occasionally be derived

from what she called "drunken oafishness" — it often brings situations to a boil. Such was the case when the TV in the roadhouse happened to be tuned to the Montgomery news station that was carrying the "Miracle Rock" story.

"That Sunday afternoon, as the sun descended and the drunken lunacy intensified, Patrick Connor saw little Maria's interview and abruptly decided to get to the bottom of the Roy mystery - after all, the boy's body was found in the woods named for his forefather. Hell bent on demanding an explanation, he staggered down the road, leading his band of inebriated kinfolk from the local saloon to the home of the shy oboist. Their meandering march through town caused such a ruckus that Sheriff Hank was alerted. Someone else called the family and Maria was instructed by her father to hide in the basement until it was safe. He stood on his front porch like Atticus Finch (except that he was unarmed) and negotiated the Connor boys down to a dull roar, all the while looking up and down the road for reinforcements. It turns out that Hank had seen the TV show down at the jail, and was already on his way to question Maria when Deputy White called from the switchboard and forewarned him about the Connors.

"Funny thing was, when Hank finally arrived, the Connors had sobered up somewhat, and were carrying on a fairly civilized conversation with Maria's dad. Patrick Connor explained to the Sheriff and a swelling group of onlookers, in his rambling, poetic manner common to Irish alcoholics (excuse the redundancy), that he had seen a vision. Hank harrumphed, knowing that Connor was prone to whiskey hallucinations, but nonetheless allowed him to continue. Hank had often confided in me that the key to negotiations with criminals and drunkards is to merely keep them talking. It seems Mr. Connor's 'vision' included Maria hiding in the basement with her homemade reeds, the miraculous stone in the woods and the dead boy. Patrick was convincing, in that way boozers have of cutting to the quick in a roundabout way, if that makes any sense, so even though my husband didn't believe a word of his story, he no longer considered him a threat to anyone, except possibly himself."

Sherriff Willis now turned his attention to his original reason for the visit, the child Maria. 'Excuse me, Mr. Battaglia, would you mind bringing your daughter out here? I'd like to have a word with her.'

Maria's father went inside the house, and after two long minutes, Maria demurely emerged behind her dad, blinking her eyes to adjust to the light after having hidden in the basement for so long. The setting sun was shining brightly on the Battaglia's porch. By now a middling-sized crowd of townsfolk had assembled and were watching in silence. Her father coaxed Maria out onto the porch where everyone could see her. Flash bulbs popped and voices buzzed. Hank later confided in Armena that he was very upset with the crowd of curiosity-seekers. He was reluctant to question the little girl in front of everyone, but he realized he was caught in a situation he was powerless to change. He was also aware that elections were coming up in the fall, so he addressed the crowd in what Armena called his best 'authority-with-a-heart' voice.

"Folks! Everybody! Now lookee here. I must remind you that this here is an official po-lice investigation." The crowd was still buzzing as the Sherriff continued to speak.

"Now, I understand basic human curiosity and the need to know what all's going on in our own backyard. But this is first and foremost po-lice business, and I'm asking you folks to kindly show respect for the law and for this

little lady. It's not going to make talking to her any easier
with y'all gawkin' and snappin' photographs. So. If you
would please let us get on with our task here, I'd certainly
appreciate your cooperation." The crowd paid the sheriff
the respect he deserved and quieted down to a whisper.
When Hank finished his little speech to the crowd, he
turned around to talk to little Maria, and somebody in the
crowd started clapping. Pretty soon all of the several dozen
onlookers were wrapped up in applause. The sheriff turned
back around to quiet them and they clapped harder, like he
was taking an encore bow or something. He planted his
hands on his hips and glared at the crowd, like a teacher
demanding quiet from an unruly classroom. They stopped
applauding as quickly as they started, like somebody threw
a switch.

Meanwhile, Maria was standing there the whole
time, next to her dad, her dark eyes cast modestly
downward. She was holding what turned out to be an
envelope and two oboe reeds. Her father said, "Go ahead,
honey." She looked up at her dad for reassurance, cleared
her little throat, and began speaking, softly and in measured
cadence.

"I used to meet Roy after school in the woods and practice on the oboe. I was teaching him how to play." She stopped talking and swallowed a couple of times. She was having trouble catching her breath. She looked up at her dad and he nodded for her to continue. "Roy left these things for me to find. He whittled the reeds himself. We found a plant in the woods that made perfect reeds." She went silent again.

The sheriff spoke up. "And what's that in the envelope, sweetie?"

Maria slowly opened the envelope and removed a single piece of paper. She held it up for everyone to see. The sheriff asked, "What is that, music?"

"Yes sir, it is. This is an etude that we worked on when we practiced. Roy wrote on the back of it."

The people watching stood perfectly still, taking in this surreal scene, listening to this little girl speak almost like an adult.

"I'm very sorry, sir, that I didn't speak up sooner. I'm pretty sure the letter will explain everything." She read aloud:

Dear Maria,

Thank you for being my friend. You are the only person who was ever nice to me. Please use these reeds next time you practice.

I am going to take a lot of pills I stole from Mr. Gordon's drugstore, then run myself into trees in the woods to make it look like I was beat up bad. Maybe one of those dopes who hated me will get blamed for it.

I wish I could say I'll see you in heaven someday, but I don't think they'll let me in.

Your friend,

Roy

Armena held back tears again at the wonder of it all.

"And wouldn't you know, the next morning the rain and clouds were gone and the sun shone brightly for the first time in weeks. Over at the general store, folks were busy shopping for Windex and shoe polish, when a tourist burst through the front door and started yelling at Martha, the owner, about her faulty directions to the Miracle Stone. Martha's nickname was the human map, so when the camera-toting outsider challenged her, everybody stopped to listen.

'I'm sorry, lady, but it's not my fault you don't know your way around here.'

'You said to follow the signs to the lake, then turn right on Dublin Road, go precisely one half mile and stop, then head due west into the woods, right?'

Martha couldn't deny those were her exact words. 'Yeah, that's sounds right.'

'Well, I'm telling you, there ain't no stone there.'

'Are you sure?'

'As sure as I'm standing here. And I got witnesses.'

Martha didn't even bother to reply. She just walked straight out of the store and cranked up her Wagoneer. All the local residents followed her out the door. Everyone in town understood at once. Vehicles revved up from one end of town to the other.

The scene that followed in Connor's Woods consisted of two disparately different groups of people marching in different directions. On the one hand, scores of disappointed pilgrims slouched out of the woods toward the road, griping of their dashed hopes, wondering how they would explain this non-event to the folks back home. In the opposite direction, hundreds of us Crumfordians slogged down the worn path from the Dublin Road through the muddy woods, where we jammed ourselves around the edge of the clearing and stared at the spot where the stone used to be, each one of us lost in our own thoughts."

To this day, folks visit Mabel's on the off chance that my great aunt Armena would be there to retell the story of Roy and The Stone. Mabel's daughter, Abby, runs the place these days, and most of the old gossip gang have long since passed on, nowadays telling their stories to fellow angels in heaven. Old Sherriff Hank Willis gave up the ghost six years ago, and Armena stays home by herself most of the time nowadays. Make no mistake, she still enjoys visiting the diner now and then, sitting at that same corner table, and enjoying a cup of tea. People come over and ask politely if they might sit with her and she welcomes the company. She takes off her turquoise retro glasses, closes her book, and invites them to please sit down. Sooner or later, the conversation shifts to the story of the twin miracles and Armena is in a heaven of her own, recounting the fantastic but true story that finally put Crumford on the map: "Rambunctious was about the kindest word anyone ever used to describe young Roy…"

The Courier, In Two Parts

JUDITH

Judith's iPhone vibrated at 4:10 p.m. She stopped running and switched screens - the caller I.D. read, "out of area."

"Hello."

"Judith." She recognized the familiar, precise voice.

"This is Judith."

"American Airlines flight # 136 to Berlin, departing at 6:05 from LAX."

Judith looked at her watch. It was 4 p.m. "Got it."

"Hotel Strauss on the Alexanderplatz. Registered as Frau Anna Schmidt."

"Got it."

The voice disconnected. Judith turned and ran directly back her garden apartment complex just north of Wilshire Boulevard, where a brown paper bag containing a locked leather briefcase, a boarding pass, and Anna Schmidt's German passport had been placed between her apartment door and the screen door. Judith still had no idea how this delivery was accomplished time after time without arousing suspicion from her neighbors, especially the nosy and vigilant Mrs. Carter, the retired widow in #3 who had little else to do but spy on the comings and goings in the building. Judith's work was deadly serious, classified government business, and the prying eyes of the anti-war, anti-establishment Democrat Margie Carter were to be avoided at all costs. The secrecy and mystery of Judith's missions were a major part of the allure of her new career.

Her life was as thrilling as a spy movie, but these titillations never interfered with the gravity and seriousness of her tasks. In the twelve months since becoming a courier, she had developed a deep appreciation for the demanding, heroic work done every day behind the scenes by thousands of other loyal, anonymous Americans to ensure that their country remained free and prosperous.

At a brief recruitment session a year ago, the federal agent had explained that Judith's expert fluency in several European languages as well as Russian had attracted the interest of Washington. That made perfect sense to Judith because her family had a patriotic profile. Her ancestors had voted straight Republican for generations. Her father had interrupted his college career at The Citadel to volunteer for Viet Nam and her brother had a top-secret clearance at Raytheon's radar division. Meeting in an anonymous office in a bland building on Wilshire Boulevard, she was instantly flattered by the offer and excited to be earning almost twice what she made at Berlitz. When Judith questioned the wisdom of leaving her job so abruptly, the agent suggested she continue to tutor private clients, which would maintain her language skills, provide legitimate taxable income, and keep up appearances of a normal life.

He informed her they would establish and maintain a special account in an overseas bank where Judith could have access to the funds she earned if she needed extra money. It wasn't long before she gave herself the pleasure of acquiring certain jewelry items she had coveted for years, and, in a grand gesture of overcoming her Midwestern guilt, she treated herself to a Mustang convertible.

With less than two hours before takeoff, Judith quickly showered, applied minimum makeup, then calmly put together her low-visibility travel outfit; a mid-calf, brown cotton skirt and matching jacket that hid her figure, a pale green, tailored blouse, plain white underwear, pantyhose, and low-heeled, sensible brown shoes. She contained her shoulder-length, blonde hair in a low bun behind her head fastened with a plastic clip. A small gold cross on a matching chain around her neck, hoop earrings and an inexpensive watch comprised her jewelry. She enjoyed hiding behind what she called her *spy costume*. Her outfit reminded her a lot of the way her mother dressed back in Wisconsin. Judith had maintained a rather dowdy appearance in college to keep away the boys who terrified her, but since moving to California, she'd begun to loosen up and come out of her conservative, heartland shell. She enjoyed the tight leggings or short skirts that turned men's heads whenever she strolled through the shopping and restaurant area of Santa Monica. But low-cut or snug fitting outfits were totally wrong for her missions, so Judith easily adapted back to her bland wardrobe of five-to-ten years earlier.

Judith reviewed her pre-packed carry-on: travel-sized toiletries guaranteed to pass through security without a hitch, and an optimistic change of clothes consisting of a dark gray, v-neck, cashmere sweater, high heels, a soft, above-the-knee, wool skirt, an evening purse, and her black lace thong, just in case. She looked herself over in the full-length mirror before leaving, satisfied her athletic curves were well disguised under her professional attire. She called for a cab to meet her on the corner half a block away. Her last act before walking out the door was adding a bright red lipstick to her carry-on.

"Hi, Judith"

Mrs. Carter loved to startle Judith from her street level window.

"Oh, hi, Mrs. Carter."

"Oh, come on. We're neighbors. Call me Margie. Where you going? To your boyfriend's?"

Judith realized her overnight bag might have prompted this particular instance of nosiness, but Judith had become accustomed to lying and was very good at it.

"Actually, I'm going to visit my sister in Orange Country."

She enjoyed reminding her liberal, busybody neighbor of the several million Republicans not that far away.

Margie Carter harrumphed and slammed her window shut as Judith smiled inwardly and continued on to California Avenue to meet her taxi, slipping on a wedding ring as the final piece of her disguise. Judith reflected on the cab ride to LAX how much her life had shifted in the past year. Just as she had begun to overcome her fears and enjoy the company of men, her new profession had forced her back into the conservative clothes and shy behavior that had protected her from the opposite sex in her high school and college days. And now, with last-minute summonses coming more and more frequently, the chances of having any semblance of a social life were practically nil. In the beginning, she was willing to accept exhaustion and loneliness as sacrifices for a greater good, but after a year, she often found herself wondering how long she could endure this abnormal existence. Her last boyfriend, David, dumped her for frequently breaking dates without an explanation. That was three months ago and she hadn't had a date since. David's quiet strength had awakened her latent urges to eventually start a family, a value that competed with her secret thrill of operating near the cutting edge of national security. As her taxi sped past the Ballona Wetlands on the way to LAX, Judith silently conceded to herself that, for now, she was married to her job.

The handsome check-in clerk at the American Air Lines first class counter flashed a smile of recognition at her face but cocked an eyebrow at the German passport, wondering if perhaps he *didn't* remember her after all. Judith rearranged her hands to reveal the wedding band and memorized his name badge and his face in order to avoid his counter in the future. She arrived just in time for priority boarding and settled into her comfy cubicle in the front of the plane. She shed her jacket and shoes, put the sleep mask over her eyes and tried to rest.

She slept fitfully during the fifteen-hour journey, remembering to secure the briefcase to her wrist with plastic straps under her blanket. She ordered lunch a couple of hours before landing in the U.K. After a brief stopover at Heathrow she arrived at Tegel International at 18:50 local time, and was met, as was the custom on her missions, by a driver she had never seen before who flashed a handwritten sign bearing her assigned name. The sun was shining at almost exactly the same angle it had been the day before in Santa Monica. Judith's German was so flawless that the driver asked her what part of Prussia she was from. She responded indifferently, naming a town that didn't exist. He shrugged and concentrated on driving. In forty minutes they arrived at her hotel in the former East Berlin.

The hotel was built shortly after the war and its stark absence of style and amenities reflected the lack of value placed on charm by the region's former communist rulers. The concrete lobby was spare, the service efficient and cool, but her room was large and nicely furnished. A wide, comfortable, leather wing chair and ottoman faced the large plaza window, presumably so her bosses could keep an eye on her. All the hotel rooms she stayed in had pretty much the identical layout of the large chair or sofa facing an enormous window that looked out on the city. It had been emphasized in her basic training session that she was never to close the curtains on her hotel windows, even when she was changing clothes. Judith accepted this rule as one of the downsides of the undercover business - nobody trusted anybody. This policy had embarrassed her at first, knowing that some lascivious CIA agent might be ogling her private moments, but her fear soon faded. Recently she'd even a felt a thrill at the idea of a stranger's eyes on her body. She had occasionally chosen skimpy lace underwear for her trips with that possibility in mind.

Judith closed the door to her room and immediately peeled off her pantyhose and unbuttoned the waistband on her skirt. She plopped down in the big chair with the briefcase dutifully on her lap and waited as the sun sank in the west, reflecting off the windows of the buildings facing her hotel. The smell of the chair's worn leather reminded her of her grandfather's hunting lodge in northern Wisconsin and warmed her heart. She relaxed her mind and indulged childhood memories of fishing and cross-country skiing with her family. She remembered the evenings spent around the massive hearth, trading stories and feeling the comfort of family surrounding her like a big, woolly blanket. She regretted not picking up a paperback at the airport. On her last trip she'd had to wait five hours in her room for further instructions. It was still early, but she was unusually tired from the journey and longed to fall asleep in a real bed for a few hours before her red-eye return flight. As this lonely existence became routine, Judith learned to alleviate her boredom by creating diversions in her mind. The conflict between so much free time and a duty to lead an inconspicuous life had invited Judith to probe the corners of her imagination. She occasionally fantasized about an intense affair with a dark stranger she met in a hotel bar, but she was more likely to create scenarios of emotional security. Her favorite was meeting a British diplomat in the course of her duties and falling in love with his patrician features and his manor house in Surrey. She imagined a future as the mother of three beautiful, aristocratic children. But lately she had found herself daydreaming darkly about sipping absinthe and smoking Monte Cristos in an underground Macedonian jazz club. She imagined herself in a low-cut red dress with a high slit leading to anonymous, rough sex in the heart of a bustling European capitol. She was soberly aware of how far she allowed her mind to float, but as long as her fantasies didn't threaten her reality, she happily let her mind wander anywhere it took her. But the more her solitary, secret life exacerbated her human needs for company and touch, the stronger she had to focus her mind to suppress her baser urges. In recent months, that battle between hormones and duty had intensified.

The hotel phone rang. Judith's eyes startled open. She hesitated, since the usual method of contact was her international cell phone. She double-checked to make sure it was charged and receiving a signal – both true. She paused, hoping the call was a wrong number. The ringing stopped. She exhaled deeply. As she closed her eyes again, the persistent, quaint double ring began again. She had been specifically trained not to over think situations when the unexpected occurred, so she decided to answer. The concierge greeted her politely and informed her that an envelope had been left for her downstairs. Did she wish to retrieve it herself or shall he 'send a lad upstairs?' The thought of a lad at her door instantly redirected her blood flow and raised her body temperature. She took another deep breath and told the concierge she would be down presently. She was wide awake now. Were her bosses testing her? Was she in danger? Alterations to her planned deliveries were rare.

'For God's sake,' she admonished herself, 'You're a damn courier. Go downstairs and pick up the envelope!'

But what about the briefcase she'd brought with her? Was this meant to be an exchange? She decided to play it safe and await further instructions. Her original assignment call hadn't mentioned any return delivery this trip. She sat back in the leather chair and gazed out her window. The sun had descended behind her hotel and no longer prevented her from seeing into the rooms of the building across the way. She amused herself by searching the windows for a secret agent with binoculars.

Her cell phone rang almost at once.

"*Hallo...*"

The voice spoke perfect English with a Bavarian accent.

"First, change your clothes. Then board the eastbound tram outside your hotel in seven minutes, exactly."

Judith instinctively looked at her watch and noted the time. "Yes sir."

"Proceed two stops and disembark. A man with a red hat will say, '*Guten morgen, fraulein.*' Hand him the briefcase and walk away without looking back."

"Yes sir." There was a pause. Judith considered asking about the envelope but remained silent.

"Your return flight has been postponed to tomorrow at noon." The voice on the other end disconnected.

She checked her watch again and quickly swapped her traveling outfit for the shorter, softer skirt and sweater. Now that the night was hers, she decided to take an extra minute to change her underwear, too. Was there an invisible (imaginary?) agent across the platz enjoying the view, she wondered, as she slipped into her black lace thong? She left her pantyhose on the floor. Her new sling back heels were steep, but she liked the way they made her legs look in a shorter skirt. Her sweater was comfortably loose yet snug enough to flatter her curves. She brushed her teeth, grabbed the briefcase and her evening purse and took the stairs down to the lobby hoping to avoid the revolving door and the eyes at the front desk.

A voice halted her at the side door, "*Fraulein Schmidt! Bitte.*" She had to react. She must appear normal. She stopped and turned, smiling calmly, as if she had simply forgotten about the envelope while she masked her anxiety over those punctual German tram schedules. This exchange mustn't take more than thirty seconds. Her job was at stake. She looked at her watch as she walked to the counter to alert the clerk that she was eager to be on her way. The man handed her the envelope with a minimal smile and polite nod. She returned his courtesy, thanked him, jammed the envelope in her bag and calmly walked out the door. The tram pulled in precisely on time twenty seconds after she arrived. Two stops later the man in the red hat appeared out of nowhere with his unlikely greeting and relieved her of her unknown burden.

She was free at last. She had fifteen hours all to herself. She decided to stroll along the broad Straße of this historic city. For the first time since college that she was able to relax and take in the details of the old and new Berlin. Across the broad boulevard she spotted the grand façade of a large, international hotel sparkling with lights. Flags of a hundred nations flew above the wide, granite stairway flanked by illuminated fountains spraying high into the moonlit sky. Limousines and taxis crowded near the wide steps leading up to the entrance. Crowds of people seemed to be endlessly coming and going from the hotel. Judith observed women in gowns, skinny jeans and miniskirts. Men were attired in everything from tuxedos to sweaters and boat shoes. This was clearly the place to be.

Judith released her hair from its bun and shook it free over her shoulders. Standing underneath one of the broad sycamores that lined the avenue, she unsnapped her bra, freed herself from the straps, pulled it out through the sleeve of her sweater and stuffed it into her purse, where she noticed the envelope. She opened it and found fifty one hundred Euro notes. This was her second bonus, and more than twice the first, both awarded to her for no apparent reason. She knew she was good at her job, but it's always nice to be appreciated, especially in cash. She looked back at the hotel again with a new pair of eyes, hoping this wasn't a dream. She applied a coat of red gloss to her lips, pleased with herself for deciding to bring that extra lipstick. The soft, liquid cashmere had begun to work its magic on her bare nipples. She crossed the avenue, feeling the summer breezes up her thighs and across her neck as she approached the hotel.

The next morning Judith awoke stiffly, her mouth dry and her thong missing. She turned to reach for her bedside bottle of water and felt the cramps in her thighs, noticed her broken fingernail. She downed several swallows of water and licked her lips, trying to wake up. At least she was in her own room. But how did she get here? She fell back on the pillow and closed her eyes, searching her memory.

She recalled her initial view of the brightly lit hotel, the uniformed doorman who smiled and tipped his hat as he greeted her, the ballroom-sized lobby packed with a noisy, international crowd. She remembered maneuvering through the crush of laughing, thirsty patrons at the bar, enjoying the physical contact with so many strangers. She remembered saying '*Stoli, mit Eis*' and the feel of an arm pressing against her side. She remembered drinking in the sensation of that contact for a moment before she turned and looked up at him. His black hair was combed straight back, his eyes were pale blue, his cheekbones sharp and wide. He smiled at her. She liked that he was tall; it made her feel more feminine, more vulnerable. He smelled of shave cream and tobacco. With a tony yet masculine British accent, he ordered a scotch and soda and leaned against the bar. Sometime between the intoxicating initial view of his noble brow and the bottom of her third vodka, the man who may have said his name was Bruno transported her to a land of sensual delights and fantasies fulfilled. A smile opened her face as she tried to focus the lens of her memory: she recalled dancing close in his arms, the chilling warmth of iced alcohol in her throat, the strength of sinewy muscles under his shirt. She remembered him whispering close in her ear in the hotel elevator. She sighed as she remembered the gentle coarseness of his beard as she held him tight and writhed through the first of countless climaxes. The memory was the most intense and romantic feeling of her life, and she wanted to close her eyes and relive the night over and over. He had even escorted her back to her own hotel.

But who was this mysterious Bruno? Could she be pregnant? Had her bosses been watching her all along? Judith had no time to retrace her steps and investigate, her plane was leaving at noon. But what about the money? She snapped out of her sexual/romantic hangover and found her purse on the chair. The 5000 Euros were in the envelope just as she'd last seen them. She tucked that deeper inside her bag and prepared to leave. A bracing cold shower returned her completely back to the present moment. She donned the stifling pantyhose and the rest of her boring business traveler costume. The final touch was plaiting her hair into a modest braid. She picked up a German translation of *One Hundred Years of Solitude* at the airport, and soon American Airline's lush, first class reclining seats were caressing her back to dreamland where her subconscious revisited the previous night over and over again. Her body felt more alive than it had in months.

That night Judith would sleep off her minor case of jet lag alone in her own bed, continuing to recall and relive the heights of pleasure from her surprising, orgasmic night in Berlin. The next morning she would add her bonus to her safe deposit box and an hour later be enjoying a vanilla latte in her favorite café on the Third Street Promenade, one more attractive single woman in Santa Monica. She would glance at her fellow coffee lovers, the students, shoppers and unemployed actors at the tables around her, and wish she could tell someone.

RICHARD

Richard watched through the tinted windows of his Porsche 911 as Judith jogged along San Vicente Boulevard. In her stretch yoga pants, halter top, baseball cap and ponytail, she was hardly the same woman who could pass for a timid librarian when she was on a mission. He pushed the phone button on the steering wheel and said, "Call Judith." He never tired of seeing her reaction to the ring and the "out of area" screen, and, most of all, how she shifted gears so quickly and efficiently when she received his instructions. He'd known since college that she was crackerjack smart and a late bloomer, the perfect profile for her job as a courier. He'd always seen her as a person worth knowing and hoped that one day she would break free from the stifling ideas inherited from her conservative family. Richard was doing his best to make that happen sooner than later. All his hopes and dreams aside, he knew she would eventually tire of this spy-movie melodrama that he'd created. In the meantime, he would enjoy secretly observing her and manipulating her evolution.

He watched through his binoculars as her face transformed from the casually sexy L.A. jogger to secret government courier as she memorized his words. When he disconnected, she immediately turned and ran back toward her apartment. Richard watched her dash off as he called Margie Carter and instructed her to place the package in Judith's door. Margie was a discovery of a different stripe for Richard. She loved to play games as much as he did, especially with uptight, condescending girls who reminded her that her time had come and gone. Richard paid the rent of Margie's sunlit garden apartment, and in return she was more than happy to deliver packages and keep Judith on her toes.

Confident his plan was in motion, Richard drove south to LAX where his crew was waiting with his Gulfstream 550 tuned up and fueled for a trip to Germany. His latest toy was roomier and had greater range than the 450, enabling him to reach more world capitols non-stop, but the runway at Santa Monica airport couldn't accommodate her takeoff requirements, so Richard was forced to drive the extra fifteen minutes to LAX.

His favorite stewardess, René, was unavailable for this last-minute journey, an unusual disappointment for a billionaire. Richard smiled to himself at his problems of abundance and dialed Suzanne's number. René's voluptuousness and personality would be more than made up for by Suzanne's advanced sexual skills.

Richard was tall and rather good-looking for a computer nerd, with high cheekbones, thick black hair and light blue eyes, yet he'd had practically zero experience with women because he'd worked his butt off for fourteen years straight in order to sell his software company to Microsoft for $6 billion at the age of 31. Since then he had been enjoying his early retirement by indulging pent up adolescent urges, traveling around the globe, making love to women on or above every continent, and on or below every ocean (he owned a mega-yacht *and* a submarine). He had always been as horny as any college boy, and his enormous wealth enabled him to turn his every fantasy into reality. But even the super-rich discover that an infinite variety of women and sexual experiences no longer does the trick.

His old high school buddy Josh suggested he might want to take acting classes as a way to meet women who didn't know he was rich. Richard never understood why Josh wanted to pursue the hopeless, erratic life of an actor, but they were buddies and he was one of the few people in the world that Richard trusted. In spite of his initial doubts, Josh was right and the classes paid off handsomely for Richard. He learned to invent games to amuse himself, pretending to be different people and making up a different story for every woman he seduced. One of his acting classes taught improvisation, and that's where his creative side flourished like a wildcat oil well. He decided to take his new improv skills into real life. He invented the courier ruse with the plan to find interesting, intelligent women with shut down libidos.

Richard watched from an adjoining room on closed-circuit TV at the serious but starry-eyed looks on their faces while Josh, with a haircut and grey suit, superbly played the role of a CIA agent, explained the nation's need for loyal, intelligent people to serve undercover in various capacities. Richard knew a woman was hooked if she swelled with pride when she was told that the work must remain anonymous.

The arrival of Judith was the most unlikely and spectacular coincidence of his already spectacular life. The same personality that had rejected him in college made her the perfect fit for his new game. She'd been a deeply shy student with a double-major course load. She spent every day and night either in class, at the library, or in her females-only dormitory. She wore no makeup and the plainest baggy clothes, but her good looks and shapely body were impossible to disguise. She shot down every guy who asked her out, including Richard. He was totally committed to software research and his ambitious business plan, but the quietly stunning Judith made him take a chance. She said no. He was disappointed but unperturbed. He refocused on work and shoved her name in a far corner of his memory.

Ten years after graduating from college, she was still incredibly sexy and less conservative in her appearance, but her shy personality kept her on the fringes of the dating game. Richard watched on the video screen in the adjoining room as Josh interviewed her. She seemed content to live alone and making a modest living teaching four languages at Berlitz. She enjoyed the perfect climate of southern California and visited her family in Wisconsin twice a year, every year. It turned out that the combination of her linguistic gifts and her eagerness to 'serve her country' made her an easy mark. She accepted her grateful nation's offer with a fervor equal and opposite to her introverted personality.

She progressed quickly over the course of a year. Richard began dismissing his other 'couriers' one after another until Judith was the only one remaining. He thought about her all the time. Women came on to him every day and dozens of gorgeous, eager-to-please babes on his various payrolls propositioned him hourly, but Judith held his attention like no other. He found himself feeling increasingly closer to her as the game progressed. The more he spied on her, the more he wanted her.

As he settled into his leather chair next to a port side window, Richard recalled Judith's recruitment session in the office building he owned on Wilshire, and how eager she was to dump her career as a language supervisor to work undercover in the name of national security. He didn't even recognize that she was that dowdy genius from college until halfway through the interview, when the sound of her voice and the shy look on her face added up in his mind. Richard was flabbergasted at the serendipity, and barely able to restrain himself from bursting into the room next door. The fact that Judith's father had volunteered for Viet Nam was pure luck. She even mentioned that her brother had a security clearance at Raytheon, something to do with radar. She didn't know what she wanted out of life at that point, but he could see she was clearly eager for a change. Before she returned for the second and final interview, Richard had learned how much she earned at Berlitz and had Josh offer her twice that to seal the deal. She immediately became his pet project. He had watched her evolve from the conservative Midwesterner to the California girl who wore sexy outfits and makeup. Her blonde hair became blonder. She kept in trim physical condition with running and exercise classes. Richard watched her evolution for months through two-way mirrors and open hotel windows. After a year, the courier/spying game wasn't enough for him. Voyeurism was not enough. The time had come to up the ante. Richard was falling for her and he needed to make a move. He called his travel agent and pushed Judith's return flight from Berlin back a day. He called the trusted Klaus in Berlin and had him change Judith's delivery location closer to the five-star international hotel on the Straße. He wondered what she'd be wearing.

Richard truly wanted the very best for Judith, which is why he sent her on missions more frequently when she began dating Dave from Orange County, a former college football player who had become a financial advisor. Dave had the imagination of a flea, and would certainly have destroyed Judith's potential forever if she had let him into her heart. But Richard's well-timed demands interfered with their time together, and to Dave's credit, he finally broke it off, despite Judith being the most interesting woman he would ever meet in his ordinary, suburban life. In the months since that breakup, Richard had been sending her on more missions, ratcheting up the emotional tension between her sexual frustration and the moral high road she believed was her calling.

Although Richard was supremely confident in every other area of his life, his growing attachment to Judith had caused him to turn somewhat introspective. He had begun looking inside himself and questioning his motives. Was he avoiding a close connection with a woman by fucking call girls and playing voyeur games? He wondered if stumbling upon Judith was one of God's cruel jokes. He wondered if he was pulling her strings to avenge her rejection in college. Watching Judith secretly from a distance gave rise to many existential questions. He had never touched any of the other courier women. He merely enjoyed seeing how they evolved (or not) in the job. It was just a game to him. Now he was asking himself if he would ever cross the line from voyeur to participant, a question that had never arisen before Judith showed up, and one he preferred to avoid for the time being. In the meantime, he undressed, crawled into the jet's king-sized bed, and pressed the intercom button for the beautiful, well-paid, and talented Suzanne to join him.

Richard's plane landed at Berlin's smaller Tempelhof airport, and he was whisked to an apartment he owned in the mixed-use building across the Alexanderplatz from Judith's hotel. He poured himself a glass of Laphroaig single malt on the rocks from the well-stocked bar and sat a few feet back from his large window with his tripod-mounted military binoculars at eye level. He was able to observe the opposite side of the *platz* undetected from his window because of the glare of the setting sun.

Richard awoke from a brief doze as images flickered in the lens of his field glasses. Judith had arrived. One of his favorite moments was watching her rip off her panty hose and flop down onto the wide comfortable chair that was a staple in the sitting rooms of Richard's hotel choices. This was Richard's favorite voyeur experience, the moment that no one ever gets to see, when the door closes and all propriety vanishes, when the public person snaps into their private state. Richard particularly enjoyed being in on her private moments, like adjusting her breasts in her bra or pulling her panties out of her butt. It wasn't sexy to him, it was the thrill of secretly watching a person, any person, behave the way they do when they're alone. Of course, it had become sexy and very special in Judith's case. She invariably kicked off her shoes, peeled down her hose and stripped off her long skirt. Sometimes she undid her hair as well, but she must have been exhausted because from this trip, because all she did was loosen her skirt and collapse into the chair. She bounced her heels up on the ottoman, legs and toes splayed akimbo. Richard headed for the bathroom, confidant his quarry would not move from that chair until she received the signal to complete her mission.

He shaved carefully and slipped on a blue cowl neck sweater that a salesgirl at Barney's had said flattered his eyes. He combed his black hair straight back and opted for jeans to keep it casual. He decided to add a couple of twists to young Judith's evening. He called Klaus and added the bonus, curious to see if an envelope full of cash would spark an uptick in spirit and push his favorite courier to break out of her shell.

She was still in the chair when Richard saw the local boy enter the hotel with the envelope. A moment later, Judith was startled out of her sleepy state. Richard watched her hesitate, check her cell, look at the hotel phone and suddenly become calm and sit. It was like watching a performance of a play he had written. Suddenly Judith rose out of her chair and answered the house phone. As she listened, Richard thought he saw her slide her hand down between her legs. He had to back away from the lenses, rub his eyes and look again. Yes, there she was, seemingly aroused by a message about an envelope. Or did she have a secret lover here in Berlin? He momentarily doubted his knowledge of her life. Regardless, there was no doubt Judith was turned on, a good time to set the night in motion. He checked his watch, consulted the tram schedule and called Klaus once more. Moments later, as she answered her cell phone and listened to Klaus repeat his orders, Richard had an eerie feeling Judith was looking directly into his eyes across the sixty meters that separated their two windows. He watched this amazing combination of femininity and efficiency prepare for the final leg of her task. She methodically changed her clothes, double checked her hair, never letting the briefcase out of her sight. He felt a tingle of delight when Judith slipped on the black lace thong.

When she left her room he left his. He walked east toward her destination. The summer evening was balmy and clear. Richard strolled briskly, indulging another of his vices, Sobranie Russian cigarettes. He arrived at the same moment Judith handed over her parcel to Klaus's man. As he had hoped, the luxury hotel across the way caught her eye. He watched intently as she adjusted her sweater, looked in her bag and found the money. The transformation from mission accomplished to available single woman was clearly visible from thirty yards away. Judith seemed to open up before his spying eyes like a flower in springtime. When she shook her hair free and began walking across the square to the hotel, he followed.

She crossed the plaza, strode up the steps, received an appreciative greeting from the doorman, and weaved through the throngs of guests in the enormous lobby. She headed for the bar. Richard watched the happy smile of a free woman spread across her face as several men took note of her arrival. Practicing his British accent as he crossed the lobby, Richard squeezed through the bar crowd until he was next to her, their arms touching. When she turned to look up at him, he was struck by how beautiful she was up close. When he smiled at her, she smiled back. When the bartender brought Judith's drink, he ordered a scotch and introduced himself, borrowing his London friend Bruno's name. The look on her face was worth waiting a year. She even stayed in character, speaking with a German accent. They talked and drank, they danced close and drank some more. They moved to a quiet corner for a late supper. When the waiter asked if there was anything else he could get for them, Richard replied simply, "A room." Judith smiled into his blue eyes and said nothing.

The not so coincidental combination of the vodka, Berlin, and the festive atmosphere of the luxury hotel unleashed a torrent of sexual energy. She melted in his arms in the elevator. He guided her upstairs to a suite where he spent the next three hours making passionate, intimate love to this woman he'd been following from a distance for a year. She was a bit clumsy at times, but her suddenly uninhibited passion was a lesson for Richard in the breadth and power of humanity. He led her through a gamut of sexual experiences and it pleased him no end that she had several orgasms, screaming herself breathless as she dug her nails into his back. Still wobbly after too many vodkas and hours of continual physical rapture, Richard gently helped her dress and escorted her back to her hotel room. He returned to his own place across the street, physically spent but emotionally high as the moon. He paced and smoked and looked across the way at the dark window where his lover slept. His mind swarmed with thoughts and feelings and longings he didn't know he had inside him. At 3 a.m. he showered and called his pilot. In half an hour, he was on his way back to L. A. He turned down Suzanne's offer and crawled into his bed alone, uncertain, for the first time in his life, what his next move would be.

Molly

Two million Irish died during the potato blight of
the 1840s and a million more fled the famine; thousands of
those landed in Boston, settling mostly in the
neighborhoods of Dorchester and South Boston.
Generations of these brave souls suffered decades of
discrimination from the xenophobic, I-was-here-first
Bostonians, but they endured the poverty and humiliation
and gradually climbed the ladder of society and politics.
They built elaborate churches to offer thanks to God for
sustaining them through hard times, and to flaunt their

success in the faces of the old-money types who had thwarted their efforts every step of the way.

Father Michael had been guiding his flock at St. Bartholomew's in Dorchester for twenty-seven years, through the Depression and WWII, through hundreds of births and baptisms, deaths and confirmations. His heart swelled with pride whenever the Bishop came to visit in his glorious, historic cathedral, with its enormous stained glass rose window and its dozens of carved saints, whose fixed, downward stares ever reminded the devout of their mortal shame and heavenly aspirations. But the changing times were a threat to Father Michael's fiefdom. The post-war prosperity of the 1950s had stimulated a second mass migration, this time from the crowded city streets out to the relatively open spaces of suburbs like Brockton and Scituate. People wanted to own their homes and watch their children play in grassy yards, away from the grimy, increasingly dangerous streets of the city. A major consequence of that urban flight was dwindling attendance at St. Bartholemew's. The passionate sermons that had once inspired fear and decency in his working class parishioners had become irrelevant in a modern world that was expanding outside the city. Father Michael said goodbye to family after family, sincerely wishing them all the best, but the increasing number of empty pews on Sundays caused him to fear for his own future. The remaining flock were loyal and as generous as they could be, but Father Michael was keenly aware that declining contributions to the diocese would not go unnoticed. Every time the rectory phone rang he answered reluctantly, fearing it might be His Eminence calling to remind him of the bleak possibilities for priests whose parishes couldn't pull their weight. He didn't want to end up like Father Paul from St. Luke's who'd been exiled to some puny iceberg of a town in northern Maine, destined to freeze his celibate butt off preaching to farmers who cared more for their goats than for Mother Mary.

The youthful energy that had once fueled Father Michael's popularity with the congregation had also waned. His middle-aged paunch and an arthritic knee hampered his ability to get around his parish. Then a serious fall on an icy sidewalk the previous winter further restricted his visits to the elderly and infirm to only warmer days, little more than half the year in New England.

The Sisters of the Poor were also making do with fewer recruits, and bless them, they gave their compassionate best to the charity cases in the parish, offering bread from the nunnery's ovens and handmade quilts to the most needy. The remaining altar boys did more than their share as well, cleaning chalices, refilling incense, lighting candles, and cleaning up the rectory. Father Michael truly loved those apple-cheeked lads in all their pubescent innocence and curiosity. There were fewer volunteers these days as more boys defied their parents and preferred to loiter on street corners after school and play basketball on Sunday mornings. The ones that did choose to serve the Lord stood silently still at the end of their service with a little pride and a dose of anxiety, wondering which one Father Michael would pick to give that extra fondle for a job well done. No one spoke of it, but many of boys were aware of the glasses of wine and bags of sweets that Father Michael used to seal the secrets between him and his young victims.

Jimmy Donnelly had been one of those altar boys until he suddenly stopped attending mass at St. Bart's fifteen years ago. He preferred to spend his Sundays lounging at home, sprawled in his favorite leather chair, smoking Camels and drinking *coffee half*, as they call it in Boston, enjoying the chaos swirling about him created by his seven children and the dog. They called him Jimmy the Poet. He had grown up in Dorchester and married his childhood sweetheart, Margaret O'Brien. He earned a scholarship MFA from Boston College and became a writer for the *Globe* where he was respected as a gifted wordsmith destined for great things beyond journalism. At age thirty, he was Dorchester's unofficial favorite son, the neighborhood's artist prince.

Jimmy's greatest pleasure, even greater than crafting The Great Irish Novel in the wee hours seven nights a week, came from sitting in his leather chair on a winter Sunday amidst the bedlam of his family with little seven-year-old Molly on his lap. He read Joyce to her while she smiled and laid her head on Jimmy's bulky shoulder. A stranger seeing their faces wouldn't be able to tell who was giving comfort to whom. Molly was always the first to greet him when he came home from work, waiting for him on the front stoop regardless of the weather. She emptied Jimmy's ashtrays, refilled his coffee or brought him beers from the ice box. In the middle of the night, when he slammed his fist on the typewriter, Molly was the only one who woke up, the only one who approached him without fear. She didn't need to speak to him at these times. Jimmy always opened his arms to her while he blinked back tears. After they held each other for a while, Molly would ask him to sing her a lullaby and her father would pick her up, cradle her in his arms and carry her to her room (she didn't have to share because she was the only girl). He would lay her down on her bed and softly sing "Toora Loora Looral" until she fell asleep. He would always stand there for several minutes looking down at his little angel before he went back to his typewriter.

When Jimmy gassed himself to death in the family sedan parked right in front of their row house, his family and friends were shocked into the realization that the gregarious man they had loved and admired turned out to have been an enigma, a frustrated victim of his own buried rage and self-doubt. He had created a long hose out of spare vacuum cleaner parts and made a hole in the floorboards of his car to steer the noxious fumes inside. He sat in the driver's seat out in front of his house while his family slept, looking innocently like a restless writer seeking privacy for his thoughts. The car was still running the next morning when one of his neighbors thought he had passed out and knocked on the car window.

No one had seen it coming. He seemed to have the perfect life. His fellow scribes at the *Globe* were especially stunned because they had heard Jimmy was negotiating an offer from the *New York Times*. His dutiful wife Margaret didn't want to know the root of Jimmy's unhappiness; she kept herself busy wrangling their hectic household, distracting her thoughts away from signs of Jimmy's hidden heartache. Neither she nor anyone else chose to see that his convivial manner was a mask covering a trove of deep, unhealed wounds.

Although Jimmy had refused to show his face at St. Bart's since high school, his neighbors never criticized his lapsed devotion because he was the artistic exception to the rules. Jimmy's taking his own life, however, sharply divided the faithful. Even those willing to concede that artists and writers have their own morality could not accept the mortal sin of suicide, even from Jimmy the Poet. Discussions of his death were marked by equal parts of sorrow and scorn. The straight-laced argued he was a spineless excuse for a man who had abandoned his family, while the more generous of spirit pitied him as one more tragedy in a centuries-long line of ill-fated Irish bards.

One saving grace universally agreed upon was Jimmy's remarkable devotion to little Molly. The brief note he left behind offered no explanation for taking his own life, it only asked that his Sunday sweater go to his only daughter. It didn't matter, because the small, fair-haired wonder always got first pick of everything, which now included her doomed father's ragged Aran memento, with its holey elbows and Jimmy's masculine smell. Every one of her six brothers coveted that ratty old sweater, and the second oldest, foolish Xavier, tried to talk her out of it, but she saw through his ploy and ran behind her mother's legs where she could safely watch Xavier receive a dose of the evil eye from Margaret. He never brought up the subject of the sweater again.

Large Irish families increase the genetic odds of a mutt like Molly coming along. Back in the fifties, no one in Dorchester had ever heard the words Montessori or Asperger's, so Molly's classmates faked reports and tests to assure her regular promotion from grade to grade while her teachers happily collaborated by looking the other way. She may have been hopeless at arithmetic, but she possessed a higher knowledge not found in books.

She never complained, she was intensely curious, and she loved every living thing from ladybugs to Xavier, even though her brother teased her mercilessly every day for no reason (there is always one family member who is unable to benefit spiritually from the presence of the Mollys of the world). Her curls were mysteriously blond, like no one in her family's history. One of her green eyes was a little cloudy and drifted gently like a drop of oil in water. Her left leg was a tiny bit shorter than the right, making her list about five degrees when standing or walking. She never ran. She inherently knew she didn't need to be anywhere in a hurry.

Her physical shortcomings were more than balanced by her extraordinary heart. Imagine a love child of Sir Edmund Hillary and Mother Teresa; Molly had the strength of spirit to conquer Mt. Everest and the capacity to love every earthly soul. In the months following Jimmy's suicide, the breadth and depth and reach of Molly's spiritual power was revealed to the world. Everyone between Dorchester Avenue and the bay came to know this remarkable girl who held the wisdom of the universe in her.

She was always in the company of Mac, the family's Golden Retriever, the only canine ever known to suffer from vertigo. Molly and the dizzy dog were the perfect pair of misfits. They held each other up. Wearing Jimmy's enormous, rank sweater, Molly and Mac smelled and looked a little alike, musty and shaggy. It didn't seem to bother her that her daddy would never sing her to sleep again because she was simply incapable of feeling anger, even at the tortured soul who had abandoned his wife and children. It was the quiet, inner peace of this small spiritual savant that taught her family and neighbors to forgive and move on.

At Jimmy's wake, the same dark Guinness that soothed the throats and hearts of the bereaved also opened the doors to feelings deeply held but rarely expressed. A discussion over the sinful gravity of suicide soon escalated into raised voices, disturbing the somber atmosphere of the gathering. As tempers boiled over and hands clenched into fists, the front door opened and little Molly and Mac were blown into the entrance hall by a blast of winter air. Together they ambled through the parlor and headed straight for the open coffin. An enchanted silence fell over the house like a wet cloth on a flame, and the mourners' frustrated ire was instantly transformed into empathy and fraternity. They made the sign of the cross and remembered why they were there. Would-be pugilists folded their hands and silently watched as Molly stood next to her father's coffin, stroking Mac's head as she stared at the box. That moment marked the beginning of Molly's quiet influence on her world. Her benign rectitude prevented her neighbors from mistrusting and abandoning one another as their departed poet had done. Instead, everyone rallied around Molly's tranquil spirit and became caretakers and teammates.

She and Mac began roaming the streets of Dorchester. Every day she was invited into one home or another and given hot chocolate or deviled eggs along with bones and table scraps for her pooch. She never wanted for shoes or mittens. She'd been given so many crosses and medals that they overflowed her the hand-carved jewelry box given to her by her Grandma Ryan. Her shock of flaxen ringlets was a garden of bows and barrettes presented to her by grateful neighbors who had been transformed by her gentle innocence. This outpouring of generosity began out of sympathy for Molly's loss and soon evolved into gratitude for the spiritual grace her presence invoked. She was a walking four-leaf clover. A lot of people who hadn't been to Mass in quite a while began attending St. Bartholomew's again.

Molly intuitively discerned who was in need of her silent ministrations. She never mentioned the troubles or fears that beset her neighbors; she simply spent time with them, mysteriously easing their suffering and giving them a breath of hope. Her innocent omniscience mollified peoples' troubled spirits and invariably achieved their unintended purpose - unintended because Molly seemed naively unaware of the power or effects of her gift. When Xavier asked her what she was doing when she roamed from house to house in the neighborhood, she matter-of-factly said, "visiting."

Such was the case when young Patrick Moriarty caught a fever and could hardly breathe. His mother was so anxious for her frail only child, that she'd completely forgotten about Molly's remarkable successes. As Patrick's temperature climbed into the 100s, his mother prayed around the clock and even considered calling in the doctor, which she could not afford on her meager widow's pension. Then Molly arrived at her door. Mrs. Moriarty burst into tearful prayers at the sight of her. Leaving Mac to 'guard' the front stoop, Molly quietly joined the mother and her ailing son near the front window where they sat so Patrick could look outside. Molly's guileless presence in their home pierced the fractured spirit of this worried woman and began to soothe her fears. The three of them sipped hot cocoa and held hands now and then, but mostly they just sat together, breathing in the Vick's vapors and gazing out at the bare trees, while the mid-winter sun made an effort to reflect off the sooty snowdrifts and dirty cars that lined their street. As the three of them looked out the window at the neighborhood that had reared them all, Mrs. Moriarty's heart slowed and Patrick's breathing returned to normal. The neighbors started calling her Saint Molly.

Then, one day, she disappeared.

For a while, nobody realized she was missing. Molly had stopped going to school and everyone on the avenue had become accustomed to seeing her and Mac wandering the streets, greeting other stopping into one home or another. Her own family had gotten used to the idea of her occasionally staying overnight with neighbors or friends. She was just *there*, like the cold winter air and the lace window curtains along the avenue. Her meandering had neither route nor schedule, so her absence for a day or two was not cause for immediate alarm; it was accepted by her neighbors as a normal tangent to the unpredictable flow of Molly's angelic life. And then Sean McLaughlin came down with pneumonia.

The realization hit everyone at once, like a power failure. Even in this wickedly frigid February, windows and doors flew open up and down the streets, neighbors asking one another, "Where's Molly?" Schultz the milkman hadn't seen her. Neither had Nagy the coal truck driver. Groups of people spontaneously gathered and made searches of the local alleys and basements and backyard sheds, all to no avail. Old Mr. Quinn, the retired policeman with rheumatism, was the last person Molly had visited, but he remembers that she and her dog had left his place on Thursday afternoon, while it was still light. Here it was Saturday evening and not a single pair of eyes had seen Saint Molly since. Mind you, this was long before faces on milk cartons, back in the days when child abductions were not part of everyday conversation. Folks just didn't know what to think.

Meanwhile, in the modest rectory tucked behind St. Bartholemew's, Father Michael was sitting at his writing table on anguish, trying to compose his sermon for the following morning. He was aware that every Catholic in Dorchester would attend, hoping for some esoteric, divine insight into the Molly dilemma. Father Michael feared he was not up to the task. How ironic, he thought, that a seven-year-old girl had set the bar so high for him. He remembered the day he'd baptized the little blonde baby and had wondered at the time if this imperfect child would even survive, never mind flourish. Who knew she would grow up to become the spiritual heart of their community, fairly usurping his own position in the parish. Now she had gone missing and they were once again turning to him, returning to him, praying he had answers, praying he could give them hope and direction. Her disappearance had put Father Michael back in the position he had lost, but under what conditions of duress? They weren't coming to him for the simple things they had needed from him in the past – his avuncular comfort, his quoted reassurances from the Bible. They wanted Molly.

He wanted so badly to save the day. He wanted to look out from his pulpit and see gratitude in every face for his wise revelations. He wanted them to line up around the block to shake his hand. He prayed for a miracle, even though his mind knew there was no such thing. He was begging God for the impossible chance that *this* time things will be different, that the unexpected might occur. If somebody wins the Irish Sweepstakes every year, he reasoned, why couldn't a wonder of that magnitude occur in Dorchester just this once?

Alas, he heard no voices from the heavens, so he went back to the old standards, pouring over his concordance of the Bible for references to lost children and miraculous recoveries. He researched fables of faith and trust and acceptance. He prayed to Saint Anthony. Self-doubt stooped his shoulders as he wrote and re-wrote his sermon.

He wondered if this paralyzing dilemma might be God's punishment for his prurient thoughts, his minor discretions. Was God wreaking His vengeance on Father Michael for having taken minor liberties with those sweet-cheeked lads who helped him with the Mass? In one corner of his mind he felt a touch of envy for the late Jimmy Donnelly, whose earthly troubles vexed him no more. This memory led him to recall that Jimmy had been one of those fair-haired altar boys with whom he'd shared a few private moments. Father Michael raised his eyes heavenward, certain now that he was being singled out for punishment.

He had spent decades in the service of the church and yet he still had volumes to learn of the inscrutable ways of the Almighty. He wondered if his struggle would ever end. He prayed to God for a fair deal. He promised to repent every day of his life from then on. He offered up his soul and swore he would never touch young flesh for the rest of his life if only the Heavenly Father would inspire him with words for tomorrow's Mass.

Father Michael was feeling light-headed, swirling in this eddy of sinful conjecture when he heard what sounded like a knock on the rectory door. Who could be bothering him at such a time? He couldn't spare a single moment for another selfish supplicant at this grave hour. He had to be brilliant in the morning. He remained silent, hoping whoever it was would go away. He held a page from the bible in mid-turn and didn't breathe. The faint knock sounded again. Suddenly, a new idea entered his mind: Perhaps this was a message, a signal, the answer to his prayers? Maybe God would forgive him if he answered the door and forgot about himself for a few minutes. He thoughtfully walked across the small, book-lined room, torn between fear and faith, heading toward the unknown in a state of abject terror, in fear for his soul. When he opened the door he didn't see anything. He immediately thought it was that troublemaker Mikey Sullivan pulling another prank, knocking then running away—but what was that odd smell? The priest flicked the outdoor light switch, looked down, and there they were, leaning against each other - Molly and Mac. It *was* a miracle.

The sight of the nest of blond curls and that goofy, tilted dog was too much for Father Michael to bear. Molly looked up at him in that cock-eyed way of hers, like she was seeing inside his thoughts with her good eye while her other one was watching over the rest of the neighborhood or maybe just looking for a place to sit down. Father Michael involuntarily dropped to his knees right there in the doorway, his hands clasped in front of him and looked into the peaceful face of the little blond miracle worker. She smiled that Molly smile of guileless purity and the priest wept. He squeezed his eyes closed over his tears, bent his head forward, and silently, humbly renewed his vow of piety. Molly reached out and gently patted his shoulder.

"It's okay, Father."

His eyes remained shut, his head nodded. His heart was once again filled with those powerful feelings he first experienced back in high school when he committed to a life of service in the Name of the Lord. He promised himself never to scoff at miracles again. Mac barked once, startling the priest back to the present. Molly patted his head to quiet him.

"Do you have any biscuits? Mac's hungry."

Father Michael stood up, relieved to have something to do, and went into his small bachelor kitchen to fetch a dog treat (everybody in the neighborhood kept a supply of dog biscuits on hand these days). As he opened the cabinet, he thought about this miraculous turn of events. He now understood first hand what his flock had been buzzing about in these months since Jimmy Donnelly's passing. What was it about this child? The improbable confluence of her physical and mental deficiencies and her father's suicide had created this flawless, powerful force of heart, transforming the populace of St. Bartholomew's into believers once again. He proffered the dog treat to Mac, but Molly took it from his hand and broke it in two, feeding Mac one piece and putting the other half in her skirt pocket.

"Mac and I have to go see Sean McLaughlin now." She smiled. "G'night, Father. See you at mass tomorrow."

Father Michael stood speechless as the two of them turned and ambled down the flagstone path toward the rectory gate.

Made in the USA
Las Vegas, NV
14 July 2021